TREE GIRL

Books by

BEN MIKAELSEN

RESCUE JOSH MCGUIRE
SPARROW HAWK RED
STRANDED
COUNTDOWN
PETEY
TOUCHING SPIRIT BEAR
RED MIDNIGHT

TREE GIRL

BEN MIKAELSEN

rayo

HarperTempest
An Imprint of HarperCollins*Publishers*

Rayo is an imprint of HarperCollins Publishers.

Tree Girl

www.harpertempest.com

Library of Congress Cataloging-in-Publication Data
Mikaelsen, Ben, 1952–
Tree Girl / Ben Mikaelsen.—1st ed.

p.   cm.

Summary: When, protected by the branches of one of the trees she loves to climb,
Gabriela witnesses the destruction of her Mayan village and the murder of nearly all
its inhabitants, she vows never to climb again until, after she and her traumatised
sister find safety in a Mexican refugee camp, she realizes that only by climbing and
facing their fears can she and her sister hope to have a future.

ISBN 0-06-009004-9 — ISBN 0-06-009005-7 (lib. bdg.)

1. Mayas—Juvenile fiction. [1. Mayas—Fiction. 2. Sisters—Fiction.

3. Refugees—Fiction. 4. Indians of Central America—Guatemala—Fiction.

5. Guatemala—Fiction.] I. Title.

PZ7.M5926Tr 2004+   2003018702

[Fic]—dc22

Typography by Lizzy Bromley

1 3 5 7 9 10 8 6 4 2

First Edition

This book is dedicated to the real Tree Girl,
who courageously shared her difficult story with me.
She did so through many tears, from the protection
of a safe house, during a long Guatemala night.
Her true experiences inspired this story.

TREE GIRL

CHAPTER ONE

For as long as I can remember, trees have coaxed me to their branches in the same way light tempts a moth near on a dark night. My Mamí told me that even before I learned to walk, I pushed away from the safety of her arms and crawled alone to a great *encino* tree near our thatched-roof home. I sat beneath the tree and gazed up at the branches as if their leaves had called to me. As I grew, I pulled myself up among those same branches and stared even higher, hearing new voices.

"Gabriela, when you climb a tree, it takes you closer to heaven." Mamí encouraged me as each month I climbed still higher. And I believed her. By the time I turned ten, I could climb to the top of any tree—even those that offered me only a few branches. Always I kicked off my sandals and socks at the bottom so that my toes could feel the coarse bark and find the hidden footholds. When I crawled very high, higher than even the boys dared, I closed my eyes and reached one hand over my head. If I held my breath and spread my fingers wide apart, I could feel the clouds.

The *cantón* where I lived was nothing more than a simple cluster of wood-planked huts that formed a small village, each home joined to the next by roaming children and pecking chickens who ignored boundaries.

"Climbing a tree is dangerous, Gabriela," the old women who lived in our cantón scolded me. But they worried only because they loved me and because they wished me no harm. Trees could be dangerous. If you didn't respect them and hold tightly to their branches, you could fall and be hurt. But Mamí knew I respected trees. Her only warning was "Hold on to your dreams as tightly as you hold to the branches, Gabi."

I was too young then to know how dangerous it would be to lose hold of my dreams. But I do remember well one day when I was fourteen, the day everyone in our Guatemalan cantón began calling me Tree Girl, or *Laj Ali Re Jayub* in my native language, Quiché. Even the boys who had called me Goat Face because I was not very beautiful, even they began calling me Tree Girl.

It began innocently enough.

I was sitting beneath a small twisted cedar tree, weaving a special *huipil*, the blouse that I planned to wear for my *quinceañera*, the day when I turned fifteen. On that special day, I would become a woman and be expected to behave as one, no longer wearing socks like a child. On my quinceañera I would dress up like a bride for the priest to bless me. Mamí would cook a big meal, and Papí would give me a wrapped gift. We would celebrate my entrance into womanhood with the whole cantón.

The old huipil I usually wore had only red and black flowers, but this new huipil I wove especially for my quinceañera, with blue, red, yellow, and green, and the ancient symbols of my people, the Maya. Mamí had taught me the meaning of the special symbols: animals and faces, squares, triangles, all telling of our beliefs, of the ancients, and of my ancestors. The symbols held the history of my people and told who I was. The huipil might someday be given to my children.

To weave the special huipil, I anchored the hand loom to a small cedar tree and leaned back against a waist strap to keep the colorful threads tight and straight while I worked. That's how I was seated when two boys discovered me alone in the forest a short distance from our cantón.

I didn't recognize the older boys. They were big, with clumsy steps and glassy eyes. When they kneeled beside me, I smelled on their breath the alcohol we called *boj*, a strong fruit liquor made in the cantóns. Both boys joked and teased me, their stares making me uncomfortable.

I felt the way any girl would, alone with boys who can't be trusted, and I was ready when they began touching me and pulling at my huipil and my *corte*, the wrap-around skirt that I wore. "You're very beautiful,"

4

one said. "Quit weaving and give us a little kiss."

I didn't want to kiss the boys. Why would they want to kiss someone the other boys called Goat Face? I shook my head and kept weaving, but the boys were drunk. "Come with us," one insisted. "You're so beautiful. We'll treat you like a princess."

The boys were blind to beauty. Their eyes held the look of stray dogs who see food they think can be stolen. I kept weaving and said nothing, but then suddenly one of them grabbed at my huipil and squeezed one of my breasts. As quickly as a cat, I bit his arm and rolled free from the strap that held me to my loom.

The boy howled with pain as I jumped to my feet and ran. I didn't run because I feared the boys. I could bite and kick like a donkey if cornered. I had a better plan and I ran toward a large avocado tree that I had climbed many times. Even at night I could climb that tree faster than the moon shadow of a passing cloud.

The boys jumped to their feet and chased me, their anger demanding more than kisses. Purposely I slowed to make them think they could catch me. They were only steps behind when I reached the tree, but that was all I needed to climb above their heads to safety. The tree reached out its branches to me as I climbed, taking my hands and helping me to escape the ground. Each branch lifted me safely to the next, passing me higher and higher.

The boys swore loudly as they scrambled after me. "We didn't hurt you," one shouted.

"You bit me, you ugly toad!" the other growled.

I kept climbing.

The boys kept shouting angry threats as they climbed farther up into the tree after me. When we had crawled high enough for the wind to sway the branches, they paused to look back at the ground and their voices weakened. The cowards didn't like being so high, and suddenly their angry threats turned to empty chattering like two scared monkeys.

"Come down, you ugly toad, or we'll hurt you," one shouted.

Now it was my turn to laugh. "What's wrong?" I called down. I spoke sweetly, the way a mother talks to a baby. "You said I was beautiful. Do I look so different up in a tree? What's wrong? Are you afraid to climb as high as an ugly toad?"

The boys' angry faces reddened like peppers as they stared up at me. To coax them even higher, I swung my feet in front of their faces, letting them almost catch me. I hoped their anger would make them even more foolish.

When the boys stopped climbing again, I reached out and picked several hard, unripe avocados and threw them like rocks, hitting their heads. They screamed with pain and swore and reached up to try and grab me, but I crawled even higher. Now I was up higher than I had ever climbed before. The branches in my hand were no larger than broomsticks. With the extra weight, the tree bent dangerously.

One of the boys reached for an avocado to throw back at me, so I held tightly to the tree and swung my body from side to side. The tree swayed as if the earth were moving. The boy dropped the avocado, and he and his friend clung desperately to the tree, their faces pale.

I hoped the thin branches were strong enough to hold a short fourteen-year-old girl and two drunk and angry boys. One started to crawl back toward the ground, so I swung the tree harder. Once more they both clung to the branches as if held by glue. The fear that froze their bodies made them my prisoners. "Move and I'll swing even harder," I warned them.

Already the sun hovered low over the trees. I knew that if I didn't return to the cantón by sunset, Mamí would come into the forest calling my name softly. "Gabriela," she would call. "Come home now. Your mothers, the earth and me, we're waiting for you. Come home now, Gabi."

Always, when I heard Mamí's voice, I would climb from my tree as quickly as any monkey. Those days when I had climbed very high among the branches and needed more time to crawl down, Mamí's sweet voice would float through the trees a second time like a song: "Come now, Gabi. Come home, my daughter. Even dreamers need sleep."

The day the boys chased me, I didn't need to wait for Mamí. A sound from below caught my attention. There, on the trail nearby, walked Don Guillermo, an old man who lived near our cantón. He moved deliberately, his body bent forward against a head strap that bore the weight of a large bag of corn on his back.

Don Guillermo had heard the boys shouting and cursing. He dropped the heavy load from his shoulders to come and investigate. I think he knew when he found us what had happened, but to make sure, I called out to him. "Don Guillermo, the boys don't think I'm as beautiful now as when they caught me alone weaving. Now they don't think I'm as beautiful as when they grabbed me and chased me. When you get back to the cantón, please tell my father and mother to come here. I want them to meet these brave boys."

Don Guillermo frowned. "It isn't safe to leave you alone, Gabriela," he called.

I laughed and yelled, "I'm not alone. The boys are with me. They're the ones who might fall."

The old man chuckled and swung his bundle onto his back again, continuing toward the cantón less than one kilometer away.

Now the boys tried desperately to crawl down from the tree and escape, but even stupid boys know not to let go of a tree that swings and bends and threatens to break with each movement.

"Quit swinging the tree," pleaded the boy who had grabbed at me. "Let us down, and I won't tell anybody that you bit me."

I laughed loudly. "When my parents come, I'll be the first to tell them I bit you and why I bit you. I'll quit swinging only if you don't move. If you even pick your nose, I'll swing this tree so hard you'll both fall like piñatas to the ground."

The boys looked up at me in silence with scared eyes and waited obediently until my parents arrived along with half of the cantón. Word had spread faster than fire, and some villagers even left their fields so that they could see the two boys I had trapped in the tree. Everyone on the ground picked up sticks and waited.

"Climb down," I ordered the boys.

They looked at the waiting crowd below and hesitated. I held up a hard avocado as if to throw it, and they began descending.

On the ground, my brother Jorge stood boldly in front of everyone else, waiting with the biggest stick. Jorge always felt he needed to protect me. No boy had ever dared to tease me when Jorge was near.

When the two boys reached the ground, Jorge and the others beat them hard before allowing them to escape. I doubted they would ever return to our cantón. Humiliation was not a poison that cowards needed to taste twice.

"Come down, Laj Ali Re Jayub," one of the men called to me. "You're safe now."

I had been safe even before everyone else arrived, so I smiled to myself as I crawled slowly from the tree. I liked the name Tree Girl. When I reached the ground, I glanced back up into the branches and felt the twinge of sadness one feels when leaving a close friend.

As we returned to the cantón, Mamí stopped to pick a red Christmas flower. She tucked it gently into my hair. "Have you done your schoolwork, Gabi?" she asked.

"Yes," I answered truthfully. "I've memorized my lessons."

I was the only child my parents could afford to send to school, and they worked harder than other

11

parents in our cantón so I could have the opportunity to learn. Though they had never gone to school themselves, my parents possessed a dignity and wisdom that I respected.

"I don't want you to just memorize your lessons," Papí said to me as we walked toward the cantón. "I want you to understand them as well. Then you can explain what you've learned to the rest of us. If all you are going to do is learn to repeat your lessons, I might as well send a parrot to school."

"I try to understand what I learn," I assured him.

Papí smiled patiently before answering. "You're Maya, Gabi, and your world is changing even as we speak. You must learn to survive change or you'll be destroyed by it. Your education will teach you how to survive. Sending you to school has given our family hope. Someday you must come back and teach the rest of us. Promise your Mamí and me that you will."

"I will," I promised. Hesitantly, I asked, "Why did you choose me instead of Jorge, when he's the oldest?" As much as he loved me, I knew that Jorge had felt betrayed and hurt that he was not the one.

Mamí smiled gently. "It's because you think differently than the other children, Gabi. You look up at the sky when the other children stare at the ground. Why do you think you love to climb trees? You see beauty the other children are blind to. You ask questions the other children in the cantón never think to ask. You sing and dream and love poetry. We never taught you those things. You have a gift, and that gift must be shared. In your heart you're a teacher. Even as a young child, each time you learned how to do something new I would catch you trying to teach someone else how to do it." Mamí paused and then added, "You're also brave, Gabi."

I nodded. Few things frightened me, but I didn't know if that meant I truly had courage. I did know the gift Mamí spoke of; it was like a quiet and patient voice inside of me, telling me things I didn't think the other children heard. The voice made me question who I was and what I was becoming. It made me impatient.

We walked in silence the rest of the distance to the cantón. That day was not the first time my parents had spoken of changes that were coming, though they always refused to say what those changes might be. I could sense their fear growing like a great storm building on the distant horizon, and I wondered what sort of danger was coming.

All my life our cantón had known only the seasons and the changing of night and day to mark the passing of time. We understood that time came to us as a gift. There was no reason to rush and make changes. We had today what our ancestors had, and that was enough. Tomorrow would arrive when it was ready. Why should that change?

Mother turned to me as we reached our small home in the cantón. "You weren't afraid of the boys, were you, Gabi?"

I shook my head. "They were cowards."

"Remember, Gabi," Mamí said, her voice fearful and filled with warning. "Cowards can be very dangerous when they have guns."

"The boys didn't have guns," I said.

"No, but soldiers and guerrillas do. Gabriela, war is coming to our great country."

CHAPTER TWO

I think my youth allowed me to ignore the possibility of war, although I, too, had seen more military trucks passing by me on the highway as I walked to school each day down in the valley. Patrols of soldiers had begun crossing the hillsides, sometimes stopping in our cantón to ask questions. Guerrillas without uniforms also questioned us.

Both sides used the same words. "You must not help the enemy," they warned us. "If you do, then you are also the enemy."

"When did you see the enemy, and how many were there?" they asked us.

"You are not sharing any food with the enemy, are you?"

"What direction was the enemy going, and what weapons did they carry?"

We could have easily answered these questions, because each day we worked near the fields, not always looking at the ground. We saw guerrilla and troop movements, and often we knew which way they traveled and where they stayed at night. But we learned to say nothing. If we helped either side, that made us somebody else's enemy.

And yes, we heard that some cantóns took payments in trade for information. Some even hid guerrillas in their homes. This carried great risks. We heard of people disappearing from their homes in the middle of the night.

I saw all the same things my parents saw, but I doubted that the changes they feared would lead to war. I wanted to believe that the troop movements were normal and that the guerrillas were simply a new political party. Always in our country there were political problems. Political parties in Guatemala were

16

never above using threats, abductions, and assassinations. But that didn't mean war.

Maybe I refused to be concerned because my quinceañera celebration was near and I wanted nothing to wreck my special day. Each day teased me with hope and anticipation, until I was ready to burst with excitement. So I chose to ignore the worry in my parents' voices. It was simply the fretting of adults, I told myself.

Finally April arrived, and one week before my birthday, Papí walked with me to each home in our cantón and announced, "Next Tuesday my daughter, Gabriela, she will be fifteen years old. Will you please join us on that special day to celebrate her quinceañera?"

All week we readied ourselves for the celebration. Uncle Raphael provided a pig to be roasted, and Papí arranged to have a priest come to the cantón. The twins, Antonio and Julia, were eleven years old and handled the arrival of my quinceañera differently.

Julia came to me and announced, "I'll keep the floor and the yard swept, I'll tie the dogs up, and I'll watch Alicia and Lidia. That will help you to prepare."

True to his nature, my brother Antonio helped with anything if asked. He was honest and hardworking like his twin sister, but he was a timid person and feared taking risks. He would laugh and clap when another boy did something mischievous like holding on to a cow's tail, but he never allowed himself to grab hold.

Though he was shy, I knew Antonio was proud of me. "You are the first sister of mine to have a quinceañera," he kept saying.

My brother Lester was thirteen and the laziest of our family. He also was the most impulsive and short-tempered. He announced again and again, "I'll make sure nobody forgets anything."

I knew Lester's voice held not one grain of sincerity. Lester always disappeared at the first hint of work. Two days before the celebration, Jorge needed help butchering the pig that Uncle Raphael gave us. He found Lester throwing corn husks at the dogs. "Would you help me to dip the pig in boiling water and scrape the skin?" he asked.

Suddenly Lester held his stomach with his hands.

"I wish I could help you, but something I ate is making me sick. I better go lie down."

Papí heard Lester's excuse and laughed. "You aren't my child," he joked. "You were sired by a sloth."

We all laughed, which only made Lester angry.

"I'll help you," I offered.

"I need someone big and strong to help me boil the pig," Jorge said, knowing that I resented such words.

I could do anything Jorge could, and more. I could weave, pick herbs, and climb trees higher than he could. Jorge's teasing came mostly from his disappointment and frustration that Mamí and Papí had chosen their oldest daughter and not him, their oldest child, as the one who would attend school. Papí needed Jorge's help in the fields during planting and harvest, and Jorge was sixteen and as strong as a small ox.

I waited until Jorge could find no one else to help him, then grudgingly he allowed me to go with him to where the big barrel of water heated over the fire.

"I'll kill the pig," he announced, as if that made

him more important.

I didn't mind. I helped to hold the struggling pig, but I looked away when Jorge cut its throat with his machete. Once the pig lay dead, we dipped it into the boiling water to make the hair shave easily. As I helped to gut and dress the animal, an awkward silence hung between Jorge and me. I broke it by saying, "Maybe next year you, too, can attend school."

"Mamí and Papí don't send me to school," Jorge answered, "because they know I'm already smart."

I knew how much Jorge wished to attend school, so I resisted making any clever reply. Jorge had a good heart, and he had come to my rescue many times. So I ignored his words and offered only a quiet smile. This, however, probably bothered him worse than any sharp words I might have spoken.

All afternoon I helped with the pig until it was scraped and ready to cook. By some miracle, Lester's stomachache disappeared when he saw we were done.

The day before my quinceañera, I found myself getting short with my youngest sisters, Lidia and Alicia. They kept wandering away, and then everybody had to stop working to look for them.

"Julia, you promised to watch them," Mamí scolded.

Julia nodded obediently. "Yes, Mamí, from now on they'll stay close."

When Julia returned with the girls, I heard her say to them, "This morning I saw a big dog walking beside the fields. He had a little girl's dress hanging from his teeth, and he looked hungry."

Lidia and Alicia ran to my side and remained close for protection the rest of the afternoon.

The night before the celebration, Antonio and Julia made decorations with flowers and corn husks. I washed and tried on the colorful huipil I had woven specially for the day. Julia began following me around and braided my hair whenever I stopped moving for even a few seconds. Little Alicia insisted on helping. I knew that the next morning it would be Mamí who braided my hair before the ceremony.

I spent much of that last evening helping Mamí cook up fresh tortillas. I also helped her kill six chickens and make chicken soup.

21

As we cooked, Alicia stayed near, offering suggestions. "I think you should do it this way," she insisted, pushing her fat little hands into whatever we did.

"Thank you for the help, my *bebe*," Mamí kept saying.

Lidia sat politely by the table and asked questions. "What would happen if you didn't put water in the tortillas? What would happen if the soup boiled too long?"

Mamí patiently answered each question.

"Can you teach a boy to cook?" I asked.

Mamí smiled kindly and said, "Love doesn't wear only a corte. It's easy to mix a recipe and to light a fire, but cooking with love is what makes food good."

Love was what Mamí gave me, not only when she patiently struggled to teach me to cook but also when we cleaned a chicken or worked grinding corn for tortillas. She taught me love when she taught me to weave the brightly colored huipil I would soon wear as a young woman. Love is the lesson she taught me as each day began and before each day ended.

She also taught me kindness. "Kindness is more

important than love," she reminded me. "Kindness is the sharing of love." Even with the feeding of the pigs, Mamí taught me to be kind.

That last evening before my birthday, the slaughtered and dressed pig was placed over hot coals to be roasted by young men, who stayed up all night and shared both the turning of the pig and the drinking of great quantities of boj. The boj helped to pass the long hours of darkness. I called it "song juice," because it made the young men sing boisterous songs of lost love and of brave adventures. Jorge, being sixteen now, insisted this year on helping with the roasting of the pig.

Mamí reluctantly agreed. "I'll beat the hair off your head with a stick if I catch you drinking any boj," she warned him.

"I won't drink any," Jorge promised, but I saw him sneaking quick gulps when he thought no one watched. I think Mamí saw him, too, but she knew that helping the young men roast the pig and drinking a little boj was as much a part of growing up and coming of age as my quinceañera.

I don't think I slept at all the night before the celebration. "What if the priest doesn't come?" I fretted to Mamí when I first arose. "What if the pig isn't finished cooking? What if my teacher from the school, Manuel Quispe, can't find our home? He's never been here before."

"Everything will be okay," Mamí comforted me.

As Mamí promised, by noon my teacher, Manuel Quispe, arrived. The priest arrived on horseback a short time later. The young men announced that the pig was close to being cooked, and soon everyone from the cantón and the surrounding countryside arrived. I was so glad to see Manuel come to my ceremony. I gave him a big hug, although that probably wasn't proper for a young woman on her quinceañera.

All of the students at the school loved Manuel Quispe. He was Mayan Indian, an *Indio* like the rest of us. He wasn't like the many Latino teachers who thought they were better than the Indios. He was a big man, big like a gentle horse, and his kindness made me more comfortable with him than I was with my own grandfather. Manuel made me curious about new

24

things, and always he made me feel that I was learning, not only from him, but from my own curiosity.

I was as grateful that Manuel had made the two-hour hike up from the valley as I was for clear skies on the day of my quinceañera. The celebration would be held in an open field beside our cantón instead of in the church two kilometers away. As the ceremony started, the priest spoke in Spanish—like most priests, he was Latino and didn't know our Mayan language of Quiché. We sat on planks laid across stumps of wood to form benches. The young men who had cooked the pig rested half asleep under the trees, paying the price for their lack of sleep and excess boj.

Papí did not let Jorge off so easily, insisting that he sit in the front row with the rest of us. Each time Jorge's head nodded, Papí elbowed him sharply in the ribs.

The children of the cantón squirmed and fidgeted during the ceremony, knowing only that later there would be food and candy and the breaking of a piñata. One boy chased his sister under the nearby trees as his mother scolded him in a loud whisper.

The priest finished his long sermon by solemnly

asking me to kneel. As he touched my head, he said, "Gabriela, you're now a woman. No longer can you think as a child or follow the path of a child. Life now bids you to share a woman's responsibility, not only to this cantón but also to your brothers and sisters and parents, and someday to your own husband and family."

I glanced over my shoulder at the older boys, who watched and smiled at me. On the day of my quinceañera, I felt beautiful not only on the inside but also on the outside. Maybe one of the boys who watched me kneel in front of the priest harbored a secret wish to someday be my husband. I glanced also at Manuel Quispe, and he, too, smiled at me. I felt my face blush.

When the priest finished, elders from our cantón rose and prayed in Quiché, chanting, burning their candles, and swinging their pails of incense and the pine resin we called *trementina*. Our religion was partly Catholic and partly the beliefs of our Mayan ancestors. God to us was bigger than the God that Catholics believed existed. We felt the presence of God in all things.

After the ceremony, the feasting began. For most

of the afternoon everyone shared the abundant food that good fortune and hard work had brought to us. Late in the day, before the dancing began, Papí presented the priest with a small gift of money and gave him some roasted pig to carry home with him. Papí gave me a set of earrings with stones as big and red as rooster eyes.

Manuel Quispe left before the dancing so that he could arrive home before dark. "You've made me so proud today," he said, embracing me with his big arms. "A teacher isn't supposed to have favorite students, but, if I had to have a favorite," Manuel winked at me. ". . . . Enjoy your evening, Gabriela." He pointed up. "Dance one dance with me up there in the clouds."

"I will," I said, watching him walk from our cantón.

Papí then began playing his marimbas, and every woman, man, and child in the cantón joined arms, singing and laughing and twirling in circles, continuing to dance even as dusk faded to night. Each of the boys took turns dancing with me, even those who had in the past called me names. On that night, I was not

Goat Face. That night I was a beautiful princess.

More boj was brought out for the adults to drink, and everybody kept eating and dancing, including the old people who were helped to their feet and moved in circles for short dances. I walked out beside the clearing and closed my eyes. Alone in the dark, I danced one dance with Manuel up among the clouds that floated like ghosts over our celebration. And when I finished that dance, I imagined Manuel kissing me gently on the forehead.

"Here, Gabi!" shouted some of the boys, bringing me a small glass. "You're fifteen now and old enough to try boj."

Hesitantly I sipped from the glass, tasting the foul liquid for the first time. My mouth burned and my ears warmed. Blushing, I handed the glass back to the boys. "The rest is for you," I said, thanking them with a smile.

I also took time to thank each of the elders for sharing my special day with me.

"Of all the young people in the cantón, you're our favorite," Señora Alvarez kept repeating. "You'll do great things with your life."

"Oh, I think you say that to everyone," I kidded her.

"Oh, no," she insisted. "You have dreams."

That night, I was so proud to be Gabriela Flores. The future was as bright as a glowing sunrise. No one could ask for better parents or family than I had, and who could ask for a teacher more kind and wise than Manuel Quispe? On this day I had become a woman, so I danced late into the night, even allowing myself a few more sips of boj.

At that moment I looked toward my future like a child watching the smooth surface of a great river. I did not realize that there were powerful currents ready to pull at anyone who tried to cross to the other side. That night, celebrating in the cantón, I sat only beside the shore of life and skipped rocks and threw flowers into the ripples, making childish wishes. For many long hours I danced and enjoyed myself.

But then Papí suddenly stopped playing the marimbas, and the dancing ceased as if by command. The sudden silence made all of us turn to look. Eight soldiers in uniform appeared like ghosts out of the darkness, their rifles pointed toward us.

CHAPTER THREE

It was late when the soldiers arrived, and very few women and children remained at the celebration. Already Mamí had taken Alicia, Lidia, and Julia back home to bed. The soldiers came toward us, most of them as young as Jorge, grouped together and holding their rifles pointed from their waists as if they might need them. Their uniforms made them more threatening. They waved their rifles at us and the *comandante* shouted, "Which one of you is Adolfo Silvan?"

We all looked at one another. That wasn't a name we recognized, and Papí stepped forward. "We don't know anybody named Adolfo Silvan. Who is this man you are looking for?"

"He's a traitor who helps the enemy," the comandante growled. "Which one of you is Adolfo?"

Jorge stepped angrily toward the comandante. "There's nobody in this cantón named Adolfo. We're celebrating my sister's quinceañera, and you have no business here."

I rushed to Jorge's side and tried to quiet him. "It's okay," I whispered, afraid the boj made Jorge bolder than he should be.

Papí also stepped in, and he placed a hand on Jorge's shoulder. "My son means no disrespect," he said to the comandante. "This is a special day for my daughter. My son tells the truth—there's nobody named Adolfo in this cantón. If you would like, there's still some tortillas and pig left. Let us offer you something to eat."

The comandante turned to me and pointed. "Are you the little whore this party is being held for?"

Jorge lunged to hit the comandante, and instantly all the soldiers surrounded Jorge and clubbed him to the ground with their rifles. His mouth bled as he looked up at the soldiers and the rifles aimed in his face. He raised his hands. "Everything's okay. I meant you no harm," he stammered.

"Everything's not okay," growled the comandante. "You attacked me." He turned to the soldiers. "Bring him with us."

"Please, that's not necessary," Papí pleaded, approaching the angry comandante. "My son meant no harm."

The comandante pulled a pistol from his belt. "One more word and we'll take you, too."

We all stood there stunned as Jorge was led away into the darkness. "What will they do to him?" I whispered to Papí as the uniformed soldiers disappeared. The happiness and merriment of the moment before had been replaced by a sudden quiet fear.

Papí shook his head, his face strained with worry. "I don't know what they'll do."

"Who is Adolfo Silvan?" I asked.

Again Papí shook his head. "I don't know. Maybe he's one of those trying to start the co-op."

Papí had told me about the co-op men, ordinary farmers like himself who were banding together with a common voice to get a good price for their crops. As it was, the Indios from the cantóns had to carry their crops for three or four hours to market. That far from home, they were often forced to sell their crops for any price that the rich Latino buyers wished to pay. If they didn't sell their crops cheaply, they were threatened.

I went to Papí's side and asked, "They won't hurt Jorge, will they?"

Papí bit at his lower lip. He gave me a hug. "Finish celebrating your quinceañera. I need to go and talk to your mother. I'll come back."

"I've celebrated enough," I said. "I'll go home with you."

Those who remained with us nodded their heads in agreement. We had all lost our taste for celebrating.

As we walked toward our home that night, my brother Lester moved up beside Papí in the dark. "Papí, I want to join the guerrillas. They're fighting for the rights of the Indios. The soldiers shouldn't be able to

34

take somebody away like this."

I knew my parents already distrusted the Latinos, the government, and the soldiers, but I didn't know for sure how Papí felt about the guerrillas. We all paused when Papí stopped in front of our home and turned to Lester. "Change is difficult," Papí said. "After so many years of being treated like dogs, many of the Indios still believe they are less deserving of respect and hope than the Latinos with their Spanish blood." Papí spoke slowly, choosing his words carefully. "Respect and hope are worth fighting for."

"Good," Lester said. "I'm thirteen now and soon I'll be able to fight."

Papí shook his head. "No number of years makes a man ready to fight. Many guerrilla commanders aren't even from Guatemala. What do they care about you or me, or our small Mayan cantón? The guerrillas and the soldiers just use us to get food and information. I don't think they truly fight for us."

"But maybe the guerrillas can bring change," Lester kept arguing.

"They're dividing us. Both sides threaten us, and

we don't know who to trust. Soon neighbors will fight against each other. Before this war is over, you'll see brothers fight against brothers, and sons against fathers." Papí shook his head in the darkness.

That night I heard Papí and Mamí speaking in hushed and troubled voices. Purposely I woke early and went to a tree at the edge of the cantón to watch the breaking of dawn. The first splash of red sunrise touched the sky as I climbed up.

I loved morning because nothing ever changed its coming. It seemed that no amount of soldiers and guerrillas could stop our cantón from waking each morning like some playful and lazy creature, yawning and smiling, content from slumber and welcoming the day with barking dogs, crowing roosters, mothers singing to their babies, and neighbors waving to neighbors.

But the morning after Jorge was taken, things were different. Our cantón rose tired and on edge. Mothers remained silent, and everyone exchanged guarded stares. We were fearful of what would happen next.

I wasn't certain what to think of Jorge's being taken. What possible reason did the soldiers have for holding him? Maybe Papí would have to go to the headquarters and pay some small fine. We shouldn't worry too much, I told myself, but still I worried.

That first day, each of us dealt with Jorge's sudden absence in a different way. Lester blamed what happened on everything except the chickens. He swore at the soldiers and kept threatening to join the guerrillas. Mamí and Papí tried to hide their fear by telling us not to worry. They insisted that I continue attending school. Julia cried, and Antonio grew quiet, standing around with his hands in his pockets as if waiting for somebody to come along and solve the situation.

The children, Lidia and Alicia, played their games, making whistles from eucalyptus seeds and searching under encino trees for the seeds that looked like cups and saucers. With these they played their games, pretending to be rich Latinos or wealthy tourists, like those we sometimes saw at market.

I couldn't avoid my fears with simple games. I blamed myself for what happened. My quinceañera celebration had attracted the soldiers. Nothing would have happened if Jorge hadn't tried to defend me. "I'm not going to school today," I told Papí.

"Go to school, Gabriela," Papí told me. "Ignorance won't bring Jorge home. He'll be okay."

Reluctantly, I agreed. I didn't really want to miss school. Two months before my quinceañera, Manuel had asked me to be his helper. Because I was his oldest student, each day he let me help teach the younger children their lessons. He called them my students, and with each passing week the children began considering me their teacher. They made me feel needed.

I purposely walked fast to school so I could arrive early. I wanted to talk to Manuel. Maybe he would have some idea of how we could find Jorge. I didn't know if I could trust my regular path any longer, so I walked on trails hidden by the trees, away from the open fields. Though I walked fast, it took me more than an hour to arrive at the school, which rested down in the valley near the river. Manuel met me. "What brings you to the schoolhouse so early after the night of your quinceañera?" he asked. "I thought you might miss school today."

"The soldiers came to my party after you left," I

said, explaining how Jorge had been taken away. "He'll be okay, won't he?" I asked.

Manuel bit at his lip in thought. "Asking a soldier for kindness is like asking a cat to bark. Maybe you'll find him, but maybe . . ." He never finished his sentence.

"Will you help me to look for him?" I asked.

"Of course," Manuel said. "We'll go after school to the military posts and look for him. But first we have students to teach."

That day twenty students came for classes. I tried to concentrate, but my mind thought only of Jorge. Finally the school day ended and Manuel went with me to a small military post three kilometers downriver from the schoolhouse.

Politely we questioned the soldiers at the military post. "We know nothing," they insisted. "Perhaps it was the guerrillas. No soldier would have done something like that."

I knew they were lying—guerrillas didn't wear uniforms and carry brand-new rifles—but I held my tongue. As we hiked to another outpost, Manuel explained to me that the soldiers' new rifles were provided by the United States of America, and that the comandantes were trained in the United States.

"Does the United States know what the soldiers are doing?" I asked.

Manuel kicked at a rock on the shore of the river where we walked. "The United States government isn't blind, Gabriela."

We did not find Jorge that day, or the next, or the next. Still, we kept searching until dark each day. All week Manuel helped me to look. The hours of walking gave me a chance to talk with him more than I ever could have at school around the other students. I had always known Manuel to be relaxed and full of laughter, joking and teasing. Now he spoke seriously. "Would you like to help me teach the older children also?" he asked.

I was honored, but Manuel's question caught me by surprise. "Of course," I said. "But why me?"

"The older children respect you just as the younger ones do, and you know the lesson material as well as I."

Maybe what Manuel said was true, but his request troubled me. "Are you in danger?" I asked.

He bit at his lip. "I'm a teacher, and you and many of my other students have learned Spanish. That puts all of us in danger."

I didn't understand Manuel's concern. Our Mayan people spoke many languages. Manuel had taught us Spanish because the cantóns in different regions couldn't understand one another. Each cantón needed someone who spoke Spanish to communicate for trade and barter. This gave everyone a common language, a lingua franca.

"Gabriela," Manuel said. "War has come to our country, and Spanish is the language the cantóns will use to communicate when they need to fight their enemies. The soldiers know this, and already they're killing Indios who can speak Spanish. You and I are among those they wish to kill. Knowing Spanish places us in great danger."

"Would they really kill us?" I asked.

Manuel snapped his fingers. "That fast," he said. "You must be watchful and careful to not speak

Spanish after you leave school each day. Do you understand?"

"Yes," I said, nodding. I had never seen Manuel so serious. His thoughts were troubled, and he spoke urgently, as if what he had to say couldn't wait.

Manuel turned to me and held my shoulders. "Gabriela, your Mayan past is not a solitary wind that blows alone in the sky. The skies share many winds. Your future is shared with many cultures. Your beliefs and customs are inseparable mixtures of your Mayan past and the Spanish present that surrounds you. To succeed you needed to know Spanish and understand other cultures."

I nodded. It was as if Manuel were apologizing for having taught me Spanish. "Yes, I understand," I said. "My Spanish isn't your fault. It was part of my learning."

Manuel sighed. "Learning that now puts you in great danger."

We wandered the shore of the river for some distance without speaking. Maybe Manuel still felt guilty for having taught me Spanish. "Manuel, I needed to know Spanish," I insisted. "You've taught me many things to prepare me for the future."

"Knowing Spanish, and knowing this or that, doesn't prepare you for the future. Your future is found in discovering the right questions and having the courage to ask them. Good questions are always more important than good answers, but it takes courage to ask. You may understand *how* you live, Gabriela, but do you understand *why* you live?"

I wasn't sure I understood what Manuel was trying to tell me. Sometimes he frustrated me. He seldom told me anything directly. He danced around with his words, making me find my own answers. "I'm afraid of all that's happening," I said, as we walked beside the water. "Is there anything we can do about it?"

Manuel shrugged. "Some questions have no answers." He paused. "But I do know this. We, the Indio, we used to have very beautiful names, like Lu, Shuan, Posh, Chep, Tey, and Catoch. Now we have very different names, because the Catholic Church came many years ago and made us change our names. They didn't like the names of our ancestors. They told us our names were pagan, ungodly."

"Was that right or wrong?" I asked, knowing even as I asked the question that Manuel would never tell me.

"Right is whatever wind you choose beneath your wings," he said. "No longer do all our customs and names come from our Mayan ancestors. Now they come from many winds. It's up to you to decide which wind should carry you. You need to decide for yourself if it was wrong for the church to change our names."

"I think the names in our language, Quiché, are beautiful names," I said. "If our names weren't good enough for someone else, then maybe we weren't good enough either. I don't think you can respect someone but still want to change their religion, their customs, and even their names. Did the church teach the soldiers not to respect us?"

When Manuel didn't reply, I broke into tears. "Manuel, I'm so worried about Jorge. He's been gone a week now. I don't know what to think of the soldiers and the guerrillas. They each say they're protecting us, and yet I'm scared of them both. They're coming more often to our cantón. I don't think we would be so scared of them if they truly came to help us."

Manuel kneeled and wrapped his big arms around me and held me for a long time as I sobbed. "You need to be getting home to your family, Gabriela," he said. "We'll look for Jorge again tomorrow." Before he stopped hugging me, he whispered, "It's okay to be fearful and restless. Fear and restlessness bring change."

Manuel's words didn't comfort me that day. When I returned home it was late afternoon. I wanted to go to the forest and climb a tree. It wasn't fair to everyone else, but I needed time to think. Quietly I dropped off my books at our home.

Mamí called to me as I left the yard, "Gabi, would you please take Alicia with you?"

"Mamí, I want to be alone," I answered strongly.

"I know you need your time alone, but so do I," Mamí answered. "Your father is still out looking for Jorge this evening. You can't always run and hide in the trees."

Mamí's words angered me. "I've been looking for Jorge also," I said. "You're the one who decided to send me to school." I took Alicia roughly by the hand and pulled her toward the distant trees. Mamí didn't understand that the forest was my sanctuary. I went there to see more than the dew shimmering on the leaves and the sun climbing into an empty sky. I looked for more in the forest than insects and lizards crawling along branches, more than woodpeckers landing to hammer at tree bark. I found trust among the trees. If I sat as still as the air, owls and eagles would fly past, close enough to be touched. I never reached for them, because I knew how that would betray the forest's trust in me, and now, more than ever, I needed a place where I could trust and be trusted.

"Don't pull so hard on me," little Alicia said, trying to free her hand.

I gripped her hand tighter, but then let it loose. "I'm sorry, Ali," I said. "This isn't your fault. All of us are scared."

"You should be nice to me," Alicia said in a loud voice.

Reluctantly I smiled. If I needed to be responsible for one of my brothers or sisters, I was glad it was

Alicia. I often felt that Alicia heard voices the way I did. I watched her once in the front yard, her eyes closed and her arms spread wide like wings. She spun in circles with a quiet smile creasing her thin lips, her little body captivated and carried by a song no one else heard.

I took Alicia's hand gently and we walked farther into the forest to search for a small tree with friendly branches that were low and close together.

"Did I tell you about the dog when he chased the rooster and the cat this afternoon?" Alicia asked. "The cat got so mad, she turned and started chasing the dog, and then the rooster started chasing the dog, too."

"And so what did you do?" I asked.

"I started chasing all of them, and then they got in a fight. They made so much noise, Mamí came out."

"And what did Mamí do?" I asked.

"She got mad and asked you to watch me."

As I smiled and lifted Alicia onto the low branch of a small tree, she wiggled with excitement. "Did I tell you about when—" she began.

I held a finger to her lips. "Shhhhh."

47

Alicia squirmed with anticipation as I crawled onto the branch beside her. "Why can't I make noise?" she whispered.

"Noise makes the animals afraid of us."

Alicia nodded and giggled and started tossing leaves from the tree. I tried to ignore her, but endless energy bubbled from my little sister. Finally, after nearly an hour of trying to be quiet, Alicia looked at me and blurted aloud, "I think we should go home now. Mamí needs help, and we're just sitting here."

Reluctantly, I crawled from the tree and lifted Alicia down. When we arrived home, Mamí met me at the door. "Gabi, tomorrow I want you to miss school. We're going to the caves so that your father can pray and give thanks," she said.

"Give thanks for what?" I said, ignoring the hurt in Mamí's eyes.

CHAPTER FOUR

The next morning, our family left for the caves with gunfire echoing in the distance. Mamí felt sick but insisted on going. She had looked tired and weak for several days. Now she coughed as we walked single file on the trail. Papí led the way, and I walked directly behind him, watching as he picked his footing deliberately on the winding path to the caves.

Papí wasn't big, but his body, like a gnarled old branch, carried great physical and spiritual strength. A lifetime of work under the hot sun had toughened and aged his skin like old leather. Living had given him wrinkles of character. Wisdom had given him patience.

Papí was a simple, honest man. He had no great vision for his life other than to be a good father and provider, and to live as his parents and their parents had. He felt strongly about our heritage and our culture, but the past was not a rope that bound him like a prisoner. He dared to ask why the Indios were treated differently than the Latinos, and always he listened patiently, sometimes smiling and laughing when I explained new ideas that I'd learned in school.

Not all parents had this courage. My friend Katrina was beaten by her father for asking new questions. She was made to quit school when she asked, "Why can't I have the same rights and respect as a man?"

Her father's angry reply had been simply, "Because you're a woman!"

Such new ideas weren't welcome in Guatemala, but Papí never treated his daughters with less respect than his sons, and always he taught us that being Indio was something to be proud of. He didn't scold me for questioning our religion and our customs.

Today, as he did each season after corn was planted, Papí took all of us up to the caves. Each of us carried a basket filled with foods to eat. Papí carried a bundle on his back that held all that he needed for his Mayan ceremonies of thanks.

Today, our hike took nearly two hours because Mamí walked so slowly. When we arrived at the caves, the younger children explored the shallow caverns while the rest of us relaxed, ate, played, and visited. Papí unfolded the bundled shawl from his back and prepared for the giving of thanks. In front of the largest cave, he lit a large bundle of colored candles bound together so that they would burn as one on the ground. Then he lit small balls of the pine resin, trementina, in a bucket and added incense.

He swung the smoking bucket in front of the flaming candles and voiced his thanks for hours. I sat quietly beneath a nearby tree and listened to every hypnotic word he spoke in our Indio language of Quiché. Softly, he chanted.

I give thanks for joy,
And I give thanks for sorrow,
Sorrow makes us strong.

Always we are blessed.
This year we are blessed
With health and food.
And now we give thanks.
Honor to the one who protects us.
We give thanks for all fires.
For fires that burned in our past.
For fires that burn today.
And for fires that wait for tomorrow.
I thank our ancestors.
I respect and hold gratitude
For our traditions.
They are hands that guide us.

I mouthed some of Papí's Quiché words in silence. The words weren't prayers offered to someone who existed only in his mind or on some cloud in a faraway heaven. His prayers were to the God and the spirits that were around him in everything he touched and did, at every moment of each day.

When his prayers of thanks were finished, Papí swung his incense bucket for a long time in silence, and then he prayed and asked God for things that perhaps no god could grant.

Dear God,
I ask for peace.
I call to the highest mountain,
And to the smallest mountain.
I call to the owner of the rivers,
And to the owner of the heavens,
Grant us peace.
I pray to all of the volcanoes,
Please bless us with peace.
All of my life,
I have come to these caves
To offer my thanks.
But I know you are everywhere,
In Cobán,
At Lake Izabal,
And in all the rivers of our ancestors.
Always I have thanked you,
For the rain and the sun,
For health and for family.

In days past,
I have asked for good fortune.
And always you have heard me.
Now forgive me,
When I ask also for peace.
Without peace,
All else means nothing.
All that we are blessed with
Is lost.
Please grant us peace.

Papí stood, tears bleeding from his eyes. He held his hands upward with his palms lifted to the sky, and with short halting breaths, he prayed.

To the God and to the Spirits
That make all that is.
To the One who gives,
And also removes.
Please take the sickness
From my wife.
She is weak.

Also I pray,
For my son, Jorge.
Please return him to his family.
His mistakes were the foolish
Mistakes of youth.
Please do not punish him so
Greatly for this.

Small rivers of tears flowed down Papí's cheeks, as I, too, wept that day, wiping away large tears with my huipil.

It was dark when we arrived back at the cantón, but even in the dark, I could see Mamí sweating from fever. "Do you want me to stay home from school tomorrow?" I asked her.

She shook her head. "Go and change the world, Gabi."

The weeks following our visit to the caves were difficult. The cantón remained busy because our hunger and our need to survive would not wait for war. Still we needed the rain and the sun. Still we needed to plant our crops, collect firewood, grind corn for tortillas, and care for the animals. Each day I attended school, and each afternoon Manuel and I walked farther into the countryside seeking information about Jorge. Papí also searched, but each passing day seemed to hammer another nail into the coffin we denied existed. We began to fear the worst.

I tried to ignore the coming and going of the soldiers and guerrillas, and the sounds of distant gunfire that drifted with the wind, but each week the soldiers' harassment worsened.

On a day in December when dark skies brought heavy rain, a column of nearly twenty soldiers marched into our cantón. They caught everyone by surprise, spreading through the cantón, pushing open doors with their rifles. The one who pushed open our door shouted, "Show us the titles that prove you own this land."

Papí pleaded with the young soldier. "We don't have the paper titles that you ask for," he said. "We're visitors like our ancestors, visitors using this land for one short lifetime. This land belongs to no one. It

56

came to us from our ancestors without any title and it must be passed on to our children without this paper title you ask for."

"You're violating the law. You have thirty days to move from this property or you'll be forced off," the soldier threatened.

"Don't you see?" Papí pleaded. "Already the Latinos have driven our ancestors from the fertile valleys to these mountainsides. We have no place else to go."

"That's your problem," said the Latino soldier. "Thirty days, no more."

After the soldiers left, everybody in the cantón gathered in turmoil and disagreement. "We must leave," some insisted.

"To go where?" asked Señora Alvarez. "If we move to the middle of the forests, soon the Latinos will come there and say we must move again."

"I agree," said Papí. "Because the Latinos suddenly decide we need some piece of paper, that doesn't make the land theirs. They cannot force us to move."

Like a family, everyone in the cantón decided to

remain. We didn't have guns, but everyone kept their machetes close to their sides. We had someone standing watch at all times on a hill above the cantón. If the soldiers came again, we would be ready to fight. What other choice did we have? This country was our home long before the Latinos came from a different land to claim what wasn't theirs to claim.

When the soldiers returned several weeks later, our lookout warned us before they arrived. We gathered and stood as a group, preparing to fight, knowing that our machetes were useless against guns. But instead of demanding that we leave, the soldiers came smiling. "We've decided to let you stay as long as you tell us when you've seen the enemy," they said. "Remember, if you don't tell us when the guerrillas appear, you'll lose this land."

I think the soldiers knew that pushing us from our land would only unite us. "What have you done with my son Jorge?" Papí pleaded with them.

"We didn't take your son," the soldiers insisted. "It was the guerrillas. They are animals capable of anything."

This denial only hardened our resolve. We would not cooperate. The military knew we feared them, and for the next couple of weeks they pretended to be concerned about us. They tried to play with the children of the cantón, and they said nice things to the elders, hoping to gather information on the guerrillas. "How are you doing, Don Rafael?" they asked one elder they recognized. "How is your sore knee? Maybe we can find you medicine if you help us to find the guerrillas."

Each child was handed marbles and candy and then asked, "Have you seen any bad guerrillas come here this week?"

We all shook our head no to these questions, even the children. A whipped dog has a long memory. We knew the soldiers only wanted information, and nothing would change our feelings about them until they returned Jorge.

Another tactic the soldiers tried once was dressing up as priests. Several men showed up at our church one Sunday in robes. At first we thought they were real priests holding a real mass, but soon even the children recognized that they were imposters. During baptism

59

they forgot to put water on the baby, and they forgot the words to the prayers they were supposed to recite. Little Alicia chided them, saying, "You didn't put water on this baby, and you didn't say that right."

The fake priests grew very upset. "Shut up! It's none of your business," they whispered angrily.

Alicia turned to me and giggled.

After the priests' visit, we kept more vigilant. We had heard rumors that the soldiers were abducting young men and forcing them to become recruits. Now guards from the cantón kept watch every hour of the day and night, and whenever soldiers were spotted, our young men fled to the forests. The soldiers asked during each visit, "Does anybody here speak Spanish?" I always shook my head in denial, but Alicia and the other children would turn and sneak looks at me. It was no longer safe for me to remain in the cantón, so when the soldiers came, I, too, ran with the young men to the forest.

Not all cantóns posted guards as we did, and in many villages the soldiers captured men and older boys working in nearby fields, and forced them to become soldiers to replace those killed in the fighting. I heard they also took away those who were caught speaking Spanish, along with those who sympathized with the guerrillas. Those people were never seen again.

Rumors and distrust moved through the cantóns like a plague. A person could simply say that someone they disliked had helped the soldiers or the guerrillas, and often that someone would soon be taken away in the middle of the night. Before long, Papí's prediction came true. Even villagers from our cantón who had lived all of their lives together now distrusted one another. Nobody knew whom they could trust.

All during this time, Mamí grew worse, vomiting and complaining of stomach cramps. Our cantón's healer, the *curandero*, came many times, costing Papí much money, but the herbs did nothing to lessen Mamí's pain and her sweating. I still attended school each day, keeping far from the open roads. Each night I slept near the door of our home so I could escape to the forest with the young men if the soldiers arrived. Always I worried that someone might tell the soldiers that I spoke Spanish. Living with this constant fear made my own stomach knot up and hurt at night.

For me, knowing Spanish became a dark and frightening secret, but the gift Manuel had given me was not a gift that I wished to abandon. Each night I lay awake on my sleeping mat, and in the darkness of the night I defiantly mouthed forbidden Spanish words.

By month's end, the military had changed their tactics yet again. In some cantóns, villagers had begun fighting back with their machetes, mounting small-scale ambushes on soldiers when they walked along the mountain trails. To combat this, the military declared it illegal to own a machete, and they came to collect every machete they could find. "Anybody caught with a machete will be considered an enemy," they announced.

Many men, like Papí, hid their machetes in plastic bags in the ground, but this left us defenseless, not only against the soldiers but also against snakes, wild dogs, and angry bulls. Even worse, now we had to work breaking corn stalks in the field with only our bare hands, a chore that left our skin cut and raw. Many nights the younger children cried themselves to sleep. Without machetes, we were like a bunch of sheep surrounded by mad dogs.

We celebrated little at Christmas, but we all hoped that the New Year might bring relief from war and fear. We prayed that Mamí might recover, and we prayed for Jorge's return.

But Jorge didn't return, and Mamí failed to improve. At first we had hoped her illness was caused only by bad water, but soon it pained her to move and she grew so weak that even standing became a struggle. Coughing and diarrhea consumed her body and took away more than her strength. Soon Mamí became so thin that her cheeks, once round and soft to the touch, grew gaunt and pale. Her shiny black hair became dull and stringy. Each night she tossed restlessly on her sleeping mat, sweat beading on her forehead as if the sun had burned her.

The curandero kept trying new cures, but nothing helped, so on an overcast day in March, Papí called all of us together. "Your mother is dying," he said quietly. "I want each of you to spend a short time with her alone."

I gathered my younger brothers and sisters and we

stood outside our home, each waiting quietly for our turn. Lidia and Julia wept. I felt scared. When my turn came, I leaned close over Mamí and whispered, "Go someplace without soldiers or war, Mamí. Go someplace where the flowers bloom brightly and where the roosters crow quietly. Go and rest in peace, sweet Mamí. We'll never forget you."

Mamí opened her eyes and smiled with thin, cracked lips. I leaned over and kissed her cheek, then I fled before she saw my tears.

Mamí clung to life as each of us visited her side. Papí visited her last and stayed with her for a long time. When he came outside, his red eyes and face were wrought with anguish. "Your Mamí has died," he whispered.

At that moment, all of us wept and the heavens cried with raindrops.

In the afternoon, neighbors brought our family small gifts, and I helped dress Mamí in her best corte and huipil. Papí built a small wooden coffin alone in the forest. I could only imagine the cruel silence that must have surrounded him as he worked. When all was ready, we laid Mamí in the coffin and rested her on the table in our small home.

Manuel came from the school when he heard of Mamí's death. He was there when all of the cantón filed past Mamí, placing flowers and beads and other items of remembrance on her thin chest. And then we burned Mamí's body high above the ground. I helped to gather her ashes and carry them in a vase to a space outside our home. I also helped to dig her grave. The place we buried her ashes already held the afterbirth of each of our family members as well as the ashes of our grandparents. This sacred land held the fluids of life as well as the ashes of death.

"I'll teach your students for you," Manuel told me before he left that day. "Your family needs you now."

I stayed with my family as Manuel recommended, and after three days, we visited Mamí's grave with flowers and candles to help send her spirit on to the next world. Papí gathered all of us that third night and said, "Don't go outside. The spirits are out tonight."

We huddled together around the fire all evening, Alicia and Lidia under my arms, all of us peering into the fire. "Let's tell stories of Mamí," I said. "Not sad ones, but happy and funny ones. Mamí would want that."

It was Julia who found strength to giggle first. "Mamí hated mice," she said. "Once Lidia and I found a nest of dead baby mice and put them in a bowl of hot water. At mealtime I told Mamí we had made her some special soup. We covered her eyes, and when we let her see the baby mouse soup, she pretended to be grateful and took out extra spoons. She said, 'I must share something so delicious with you.'"

"What did you do?" Antonio asked.

"We ran screaming from the table."

Lester laughed so hard that spit came from his nose, and then the rest of us laughed even harder.

Before the night ended, each of us had told stories of Mamí, laying her to rest in our minds as carefully as we had buried her ashes, sharing memories of happiness and not of grief. This was something Mamí had done with our family when her mother had died.

Halfway through that long evening, Papí went outside by himself. When I heard a strange noise, I peeked outside. Papí was tying a neighbor's donkey behind our home to make noises so he could tell Lidia and Alicia that they were hearing spirits.

When Alicia heard the donkey move outside, she whispered in my ear, "Mamí, do you hear the spirits outside?"

When Alicia called me Mamí, great watery tears blurred my eyes. I cuddled her closer and said, "Yes, Alicia dear, I hear the spirits." I was so proud of our family that night. Jorge was gone, and now so was Mamí, but still our family sat around the fire, unbroken.

After everyone had gone to their sleeping mats that night, Papí came to me. "Gabriela," he said. "With Jorge and your Mamí gone, you are now the oldest. I will need your help more at home, but I want you to still go to school."

I nodded.

Papí continued. "Promise me one thing. If anything ever happens to me, you must protect your younger brothers and sisters as if they were your own children. Will you promise me this?"

Promises borrow from the future, but of course, I said, "Yes," never realizing how soon I would need to honor my promise.

CHAPTER FIVE

The first rumors of war had come to our cantón less than one year before Mamí's death. And from the beginning, I had assumed it was not our war. Why would we have enemies? We were only *campesinos*, country people, and we didn't care about politics or power. We cared only about our families and raising food for our survival.

For this reason I didn't understand why the soldiers kept coming to our cantón. "The guerrillas are communists," they shouted. "If you help the guerrillas, then you, too, are communists."

In school, Manuel had explained communism to

me, but most in our cantón had never heard of the words *communism*, *democracy*, *socialism*, and *capitalism*. We wished only to live our lives and to work the same land that our parents, grandparents, and great-grandparents had farmed. Mamí and Papí had taught us to help all people, not just this kind or that kind. If wanting to live peacefully as human beings made us capitalists, socialists, or communists, none of us cared. We wished only to be left alone to live the ways of our ancestors. Why should that make us someone's enemy?

With the fighting and sounds of gunfire, many parents stopped allowing their children to leave the cantón to attend school. Papí refused to do this. He said to me, "Gabriela, I know you want to learn."

Papí was right. Like Manuel, I believed that knowledge would somehow help me to survive. I was hungry to learn, and since I had become Manuel's helper, the younger children considered me their teacher. I felt an obligation to help at home, but teaching the children made me feel needed, and I knew that working with them would help me to think less about Jorge and Mamí. Still, I stayed home for one week following Mamí's death.

The day I returned to school, I left home early so that I could prepare lessons for the younger children. Manuel insisted I spend half of each day with my own studies. The other half he allowed me to teach math, reading, and science to the children, Enrique, Victoria, Lisa, Sami, and Carmen.

When I arrived, Manuel was already at his desk, rubbing his neck as if it were sore.

"How is my teacher, Manuel?" I asked cheerfully.

"Your teacher would be better if there weren't a war," he answered, looking out the window as he spoke.

"Is something wrong?" I asked.

Manuel threw up his hands. "The world is wrong." He turned in his chair to look at me, then relaxed with a tired smile. "I'm sorry, Gabriela. You didn't come to school to hear your teacher complain." Again, Manuel glanced out the window.

"It's okay," I said, missing Manuel's normal joking and teasing. "Are you watching for the students or for soldiers?" I asked.

Manuel shrugged. "Maybe I'm looking for ghosts. How is your family?" he asked.

"We're looking for ghosts, too," I said.

Manuel and I spoke until it was time for school to begin. Only six students arrived for classes that day: Me; three older students, Rubén, Federico, and Pablo; and two of the younger students, Victoria and Lisa. I was happy to see Victoria and Lisa, because they were so close to learning the alphabet. If they finished memorizing the last few letters today, I had two pieces of candy saved for them as a reward.

Manuel acknowledged the few students who had arrived, then leaned heavily back in his chair and scratched at his head as if weighing some great decision. "Instead of sitting in a hot schoolhouse, let's go to the river for a picnic," he announced. "I'll teach all of you how to fish with a net."

I knew something worried Manuel that day. Maybe he feared soldiers arriving, or maybe other thoughts weighed on him. Whatever the reason, I didn't mind taking the children away from the schoolhouse to the river. Lisa and Victoria could finish learning the alphabet outside as well as inside.

As if relieved by his decision, Manuel grabbed

Rubén and tickled him. "What have you been eating at home? You're fatter than my pig!"

Rubén screamed with delight and tickled Manuel back. "And you're bigger than our cow."

"He's bigger than an elephant," Victoria said.

"Let's go to the stream," Manuel said, picking up a small pack. He also gave a small throw net to Federico to carry. I liked Federico. He was a tall, thin boy who thrived, as I did, on learning. He wrote beautiful poetry that sounded like gentle songs when he read them aloud in class.

I watched Manuel as he led us down the path from the school toward the river. Many teachers shouted and punished students. Manuel spoke quietly, even when he was disappointed in a student. He treated each of us with great respect, as if our thoughts were worth more than his own. We would have followed him anywhere.

As we walked, Manuel kept glancing over his shoulder toward the trees. I, too, worried about soldiers, but I had never seen Manuel this way. He seemed to calm down when we reached the river. Here we couldn't be seen from either the school or the highway. Manuel spread out the net and began showing us how to throw it into the water.

When Manuel wasn't watching, I snuck up behind him and threw the end of the net over him. "We caught a whale! We caught a whale!" I shouted.

Instantly everybody tackled Manuel, and soon he rolled back and forth on the shore like a beached whale, grunting and tickling the youngest children who climbed on top of him. Finally he sat up, breathing hard, and untangled himself from the net. "Does anybody want to know what's in my pack?" he asked.

Instantly Victoria and Lisa grabbed his big hands and led him back upstream to the shade of a single cottonwood tree beside the river. Slowly, as if feeling lazy, Manuel opened the pack and handed a bottle of orange drink to each of us. One at a time, he opened our bottles for us. The drinks had grown warm from the hot day, but we didn't care. Last, he pulled out a small bag of tortillas. "Let's have lunch," he said.

We all grouped ourselves close to him as he lowered himself down to sit on a low rock. Manuel's fear and concern seemed to have disappeared. His face relaxed, and his eyes danced with mischief as he pretended to take Pablo's drink.

We were still laughing when we noticed soldiers, ten of them with their rifles slung over their shoulders, marching directly toward us. Our laughing and joking stopped, and we waited quietly, hoping they were only passing by.

The soldiers walked to where we sat. "Why are you here with these children?" the comandante shouted at Manuel.

At first, Manuel pretended not to understand Spanish, but the comandante walked up to Rubén, who sat with the rest of us on the ground. He kicked Rubén hard. "Do you know Spanish?" he shouted.

Manuel stood. "I speak Spanish," he answered quietly. "Please don't hurt the children. I'm their teacher."

"And what do you teach them?"

"Many things," Manuel said. "How to read and write, and how to think."

The comandante who asked the questions was a very ugly man. His rough skin made his face look like a pineapple, and his eyes were small and black, like those of a snake. "To think how?" he shouted. "Like communists?"

"No. I teach the children to—"

Without warning, the comandante spun and struck Manuel in the stomach with the butt of his rifle before he could finish speaking. The soldier's large mouth spread into a wicked smile, then quickly tightened to a thin line. "Lies!" he shouted. "All lies!"

I scrambled to my feet, and instantly several soldiers pointed their rifles at me. Manuel bent over, but he didn't cry out or fight back.

"No!" I shouted in Spanish, ignoring the risk. "He never taught us to be communists."

The comandante walked up to me with a curious, ugly stare. "You're India," he spit, saying the word as if it were dirty and vulgar. "Where did you learn Spanish so well?"

Before I could answer, he slapped my face so sharply it felt as if my head had exploded. I fell over, and the taste of sweet blood filled my mouth.

"Please don't hurt the children," Manuel begged

once more, and again the comandante jabbed the butt of his rifle into Manuel's stomach, knocking him to the ground. All of us scrambled to our feet. Victoria and Lisa screamed and started running away from the soldiers.

A soldier lifted his rifle to his shoulder.

For a moment I stood in disbelief as the man aimed his rifle.

"No! Don't shoot!" I screamed, chasing after the girls.

"Bring them back or we'll kill them!" shouted the comandante.

I caught up to both girls and held each of them firmly by the arm. They trembled like small bushes in a strong wind. I coaxed them back toward the group, whispering, "Don't scream or run. Come back quietly."

The soldiers had forced Manuel back to his feet and tied his hands behind his back. One by one they started taking turns hitting him in the stomach and face. One soldier kicked Manuel between the legs. Manuel's face paled as the cowards in green uniforms hit him again and again. When he looked over at us, the tears in his eyes told me that he cared and worried more for us than himself. But we were only children. We couldn't help him.

All of us stood whimpering and shaking, terrified. I tried to look away, but a soldier grabbed me and twisted my face forward to watch. All of us were forced to watch what happened that day. Lisa cried loudly, and Manuel had the strength to look at her and mouth the words *Don't be afraid.* Then another fist smashed his face.

Taking turns, the soldiers struck Manuel again and again until their fists grew sore and their arms tired. I wanted to throw up from all the anger and fear inside of me. Manuel's face swelled and became puffy. Blood leaked from his nose and from the sides of his mouth. His eyes bulged, and his skin changed from white to red and back again.

He grunted each time he was hit, but not once did he cry out or fight back. Manuel was the bravest man I had ever known. When he grew so weak that he could no longer stand, two soldiers held him up by his arms while others continued to strike him.

I noticed during the beating that two of the soldiers were Indios. They didn't seem to delight in their actions the way the other soldiers did. They probably knew they would be beaten themselves if they refused to help torture Manuel.

I don't know when Manuel died. The soldiers didn't know either, but they suddenly grew angrier when they realized they were beating a dead man. I felt overwhelming relief when at last I realized that the freedom of death had lifted Manuel from his body and carried him up to a place where no soldier could ever reach him. Up to the place where we had danced the night of my quinceañera.

I peeked at the other students, Victoria, Lisa, Rubén, Federico, and Pablo. We had all stood bravely through the beating, but when Manuel's body dropped to the ground, we all cried. The ugly comandante tucked his shirt back into his pants, then turned and walked up to us as if killing Manuel had made him more important. "If any of you speak of what happened here," he said, "we'll find you and kill you. Do you understand?"

We all nodded our heads obediently.

"Then go!" he screamed.

We ran.

As a group we scrambled across the rocky shore toward the forest a hundred yards away, but before we reached the trees, shots rang out. Beside me, young Pablo stumbled and went down, smearing blood on the rocks where he landed. I looked back and saw Victoria also collapse in a heap, shot dead.

I gasped for air and screamed in terror as Rubén fell next. He fell hard, and his head made a dull thud as it hit a rock. I looked back and saw young Lisa running frantically behind us, unable to keep up. I slowed to grab her hand, but as I reached for her, a shot rang out and she, too, crumpled to the earth.

I wanted desperately to stop and help each of them, but in that moment to stop was to die instantly. Only Federico and I remained. Federico was taller than I but couldn't run as fast. "Run faster, Federico!" I screamed.

We had almost reached the trees when another shot echoed and Federico collapsed. The sound of each shot felt like a jolt of lightning hitting me, numbing me, making me feel as if everything was happening very slowly. I had never known such fear. My distance from the soldiers was all that saved me then, though I expected each step to be my last.

As I reached the trees, the soldiers shouted to each other and began chasing me. I knew if I kept running they would catch me. My only chance was to do what they least expected. When the trees hid me completely, I ran to the nearest machichi tree and climbed faster than I had ever climbed before. I crawled frantically from branch to branch, looking back over my shoulders. The loud shouting and the pounding of boots on the ground echoed through the forest and soon passed below me.

I sat in the tree, breathing hard and fast. Maybe the soldiers hadn't aimed at me because I was an older girl and they had worse plans for me than bullets. That thought made me even more frightened as I waited in the tree. If even one soldier looked up, they would find me and kill me. But their minds still chased a young woman they thought ran ahead of them. They were wild men, waving their rifles like sticks and shouting as they ran deeper into the forest. Their wicked laughter rang wildly through the trees.

I remained in the machichi tree until the shouting faded a little more, then I climbed down the tree even faster than I had climbed up. When I reached the ground, I ran back out of the forest toward the river and to the fallen bodies of Pablo, Victoria, Rubén, Lisa, and Federico. I rolled each body over, but no life remained in any of them. I didn't stop beside Manuel's body. I knew for sure he had joined the clouds. Instead I ran hard downstream. The dull *thud* of bullets hitting small bodies echoed in my memory as I ran and ran.

CHAPTER SIX

Manuel had often asked his students what thoughts we had when we looked up at the sky. Always since that day beside the river, I have thought only of Manuel when I look up. I see his face in the clouds and I feel his gentleness in the breeze. I feel him dancing in my arms. Whenever raindrops fall, they come as tears from a better place.

After the deaths of Manuel and the schoolchildren, word of the massacre spread like wind through the cantóns, fields, and countryside. Men from each cantón were sent to return the bodies for burial.

Of course, the Army denied the killing and blamed

everything on the guerrillas. They asked to talk to the student who would accuse them of such barbaric things. But we weren't that stupid. Whenever the soldiers came to our cantón, Papí sent me to the forest to hide in the trees.

No longer able to attend school, and with Mamí and Jorge gone, my younger brothers and sisters became my full-time responsibility. Because Alicia was the youngest and the most helpless, I let her sleep with me. I hugged and comforted her whenever thunder rumbled across the sky. She kept calling me Mamí, and I didn't correct her. All children need a mother.

Papí spent his days in the fields harvesting the corn and coffee; he had no time to leave the cantón to go to the pueblo for market. So, although I was only fifteen, it also became my job to go to market each week. The only market for selling our coffee was ten kilometers away, so each weekend during harvest, I arose two hours before sunrise and walked for three hours to market. Always I kept to the mountain paths, avoiding the military patrols on the roads.

When I arrived at market, I spread the coffee onto

an old blanket on the ground and used a tin can for measuring. I didn't have a weight scale like some vendors. This made it easier for the Latinos to accuse me of shorting them. When the coffee sold, I bought chili powder, soap, or spices to take back to the cantón. Sometimes enough change remained for me to buy hair ties for Julia, Lidia, and Alicia, and a piece of candy for Lester and Antonio.

But sometimes the coffee didn't sell and I had to carry it back to our cantón along with a much heavier burden, the news for Papí that we couldn't even buy salt until the following week when I would travel to market again.

In the market, the Indios whispered to each other in hushed tones. Some believed the guerrillas were trying to help the Indios, and they spoke of young men from different cantóns enlisting to join the fight. The military, unable to enlist many Indios, kept coming to the cantóns and taking away men and older boys at gunpoint to fight for them. Still, nobody from our cantón had joined the guerrillas.

By July, horrible stories were whispered in the

marketplace of whole cantóns being burned and everybody killed. Rumors spread that hundreds of people were dying. Thousands of Indios were fleeing north into Mexico, the closest place for them to try and escape the madness.

Still the soldiers blamed the guerrillas, and the guerrillas blamed the soldiers. I wasn't sure what to think. I heard of guerrillas who killed military men, but I also heard of guerrillas who spied for the military. Still, I believed that only the soldiers were hateful enough to massacre whole cantóns. I had seen their thirst for blood with my own eyes.

By August most cantóns had posted lookouts to give themselves enough warning to run when the soldiers approached. Angered when they discovered a cantón empty, the soldiers burned down homes.

With each passing day, the war changed around us. As the soldiers earned a reputation for being coldblooded killers, many Indios openly sided with the guerrillas.

Each week at market, I heard more and more stories of soldiers killing the Indios and the campesinos with no pretense. One week the old man selling fruit next to me in the market leaned over and whispered to me, "They're sending out death squads now to kill us because we're Indios. They want all of us dead."

Manuel had told me of genocide in history, but I never dreamed that such a thing would come to Guatemala, and that we, the Maya, would be its victims. But the brutality I'd seen convinced me that the old man was right.

Returning from market one evening, I forced myself to walk along the river where the soldiers had massacred Manuel and the children. Standing there with the water flowing gently at my feet, I heard new sounds, the drumbeat of helicopters on patrol and the sounds of machine guns spitting death. These were new tools to be used against the Indios. As I stood there, a helicopter flew low downriver, forcing me to run and hide beneath some trees.

More than ever, I worried about leaving my family to go to market, but if I did not go we would not eat. Starvation would kill us as surely as any soldier's bullet. Still, nothing could have prepared me for the Saturday afternoon when I returned home late and saw fires burning ahead of me in our cantón. A rotten scorched smell filled the air.

I broke into a run. At first I spotted only a single body lying in front of a burning home, but then I saw another and another. Scattered everywhere among the ashes of our cantón were corpses. Many who hadn't been killed by soldiers in the cantón lay dead in the open fields, killed by rifles or maybe by machine guns aimed from the helicopters. In the late-afternoon light, the fallen bodies looked like scattered branches from a tree. But they weren't branches. They were people I knew—aunts, uncles, grandparents, and neighbors.

I stared in shock, convulsing as tears burned my cheeks like hot water. Again and again I swallowed at the bitter taste building in my throat, trying to make me throw up. This was my worst nightmare.

I ran frantically from one fallen body to the next, searching for my family. I found Papí first. Crumpled in the grass, his body looked frail and weak. Not ten yards away lay my little sister, Lidia, facedown as if asleep. Two red stains on her huipil showed where she had been shot. I ran to Papí and then to Lidia, and fell beside their bodies, hugging them and sobbing. "No! No! No!" I cried.

Closer to our burned homes, I found Julia lying among several other children, faceup, a stick still in her hand as if she'd been trying to protect those around her in the only way she knew. I pulled a shawl from one of the dead bodies and laid it over Julia's innocent face.

I walked now as if in a stupor, my mind drunk from shock. I wandered out away from our burned homes, searching. Not until I reached the trees did I find the next body. Lester lay dead behind two shrubs, as if he'd been trying to hide. I kept searching, but Antonio and Alicia were nowhere in sight.

As I stumbled around in horror, my eyes burned from smoke and tears. I had betrayed my promise to Papí that I would care for my brothers and sisters if he died. I hadn't even been there for him.

Numbed by shame and despair, I dragged the cold bodies of those I loved back to what remained of our home. I would bury Papí, Lester, Lidia, and Julia in the same sacred place I had buried Mamí's ashes. As I dug shallow graves with a stick and bleeding hands, terrible thoughts haunted me. I imagined the children's terror in their last desperate moments before death, everybody screaming and running, the soldiers shouting, and the guns echoing like thunder.

I couldn't stop weeping and hiccuping with grief. Even as I dug the simple graves, I looked up and saw two more bodies of neighbors I'd known. All the bodies in the cantón needed to be buried, but I was only one person, and even as I piled rocks on top of the four graves, I knew that by morning the rats, the armadillos and the foxes would dig up all that I had buried. Even now, buzzards circled overhead and landed to pick at the bodies. I shouted at them but could do nothing more. I had no shovel to bury anyone decently.

As I looked around me I noticed a hairbrush in the ashes and picked it up. This was Mamí's brush. Many times she had used it to brush my hair. Now it was the only physical object I had left from my family. I slipped it inside my huipil.

I feared that if I did not stay for three days to take flowers and candles to my family's grave their spirits would not rise to the next world from where they lay buried.

If friends and family didn't carry their deceased to the hills to be burned high above the ground, if spirits were not sent properly to the next world, what became of them? The question cut away at my heart and soul. I felt I was betraying my family, my ancestors, and the ancients. Still, I knew that I could not remain in the cantón for fear of the soldiers returning. I had to move on.

Not finding Antonio and Alicia also hurt me deeply. My little sister had placed all of her trust in me when she called me "Mamí." I imagined her screaming "Mamí! Mamí! Mamí!" as the soldiers fired around her. Had she mistaken the sounds of gunfire for thunder?

I wept more tears, knowing I must leave with all of my questions unanswered. Other military foot patrols would pass soon, so I walked for the last time away from the place where I had been born and raised. I walked straight into the forest and headed north toward the border of Mexico, the direction I had been told that many Indios fled to escape from Guatemala. I took only memories with me, but they weighed heavier on my heart than any burden I'd ever carried to market. Behind me lay ashes of death, ahead lay clouds of uncertainty. I was a young girl alone in a dangerous country, with no home and no future.

I had walked only a few hundred meters into the forest when a whimpering sound like that of a hurt animal caught my attention. It came from beneath a clump of bushes just ahead of me. Fearing a trap set by the soldiers, I quietly lowered myself to my stomach to peek beneath the bush.

Deep under the branches, a small girl cowered on the ground, naked, hugging her knees. Beside her crouched a young boy. They both turned to stare at me.

My heart exploded with happiness. "Alicia and Antonio!" I gasped.

CHAPTER SEVEN

Alicia scrambled from under the bush and climbed into my arms. She clung to me with little fingers that dug sharply into my skin.

"Are you okay?" I asked.

She whimpered, searching back over her shoulder, her big eyes wild with fear, lips trembling. Black mud covered her round face and tangled black hair.

"You're safe now," I said softly, hugging her naked body close. Alicia clung to my neck as I reached for Antonio and helped pull him from under the bush. I tried to hug him, too, but he grimaced and cried out in pain.

"What's wrong?" I asked. As I spoke, I saw that the bottom of his shirt dripped blood.

Antonio grunted.

Before I could look at his wound, men's voices sounded close behind us. "We have to leave, now!" I whispered, helping Antonio to stand. "Can you walk?"

He nodded and stumbled after me, grasping his side. I carried Alicia roughly as we escaped through the trees up a long, steep hill. She weighed heavy in my arms. At the top, I had to set her down to rest. She tried to cling to my neck, but I took her hand firmly. "You must walk," I said. "I can't carry you."

Antonio breathed heavily beside me. I needed to look at his wound, but the voices sounded even closer behind us. "We can't stop yet," I whispered. "Can you go a little farther?"

Antonio answered with a grimace, and we kept rushing through the trees until the voices grew distant. Antonio's ragged breathing begged me to stop. I looked around. Here we were offered little protection. Ahead of us the forest opened into a large clearing with only a few scattered trees and shrubs, but on the other side stood a thick forest that would keep us away from the roads and hidden from military convoys. I knew that by crossing the clearing we risked being caught out in the open. But we had no other choice, so I continued on.

Most days, campesinos from the cantóns walked these trails, returning corn, fruit, coffee, vegetables, and herbs from the countryside. That day nothing moved. All life had disappeared as if by some act of God. But this was no act of God; this was the work of the devil. A deadly silence slowed even the breeze.

Antonio hobbled beside me, bent over in pain.

I pointed. "We need to make it to those trees to be safe," I said. "Then I can look at your wound."

Antonio nodded and forced a pained smile, never once allowing a single word of complaint.

I looked at my brother with a new appreciation. Because the ground here was flat, we moved faster and had crossed half of the clearing by the time I heard the helicopter. It was a faint beating sound echoing through the air like a grasshopper, quickly growing louder.

I grabbed Antonio's arm and tightened my grip on

Alicia's hand. "Run!" I shouted, pulling them behind me as we rushed toward the distant trees. We were caught in the open with only a couple of trees for cover.

Soon the helicopter thumped like a loud drum as it appeared over the hills behind us. We ran harder, Antonio gasping in pain from trying to keep up. It was almost dusk, and I hoped the helicopter would pass without seeing us, but the big machine banked sharply. I ran toward the nearest tree, pulling Antonio and Alicia along, but it was too late. The loud burping of a machine gun sounded, and to my left dirt exploded. The helicopter roared overhead, banking around for another pass.

Alicia screamed and Antonio stumbled forward, his face twisted in pain. As the helicopter approached again, we ran under a lone tree, trying, all three of us, to huddle behind its thin trunk. This time the machine gun spit bullets into the branches above us, raining leaves and chips of wood onto our heads. Then the helicopter thundered past once more.

Fear blinded me and robbed my breath as I dashed

with Alicia and Antonio toward the next tree, trying to escape the monster roaring overhead. We made it to the tree, but it was too small for protection, so we continued as the helicopter turned again to let the machine gun hammer at us.

We kept pushing forward toward the thick forest, expecting bullets to rip us apart as the helicopter passed overhead once more. But still we lived, each new breath a miracle. Now only a narrow stretch of open ground separated us from the cover of trees a stone's throw away. I broke into the open and ran as fast as I could. "Keep going!" I screamed, dragging Antonio and Alicia. This time the helicopter slowed and hovered over us, its long blades whipping up a storm of dust and dried grass that blinded me.

We ran, tripping and stumbling and holding on to each other. Alicia screamed and Antonio cried out in pain, but we didn't stop. All around us the air shook with explosions and the helicopter's deafening thumps. Chunks of dirt stung my skin, but I kept on my feet, fighting toward the trees now only a few feet away. The boiling dust churned about us, choking us, but also hiding our movements.

And then we were safe under the trees. In the gathering darkness, the gunner fired into the upper branches, but I knew that he couldn't see us. Once again the forest had saved me. I listened as the helicopter circled twice and then abandoned its mission. The pulsing of its blades faded away down the valley.

Antonio collapsed to his knees, gasping for air. I knelt beside him and lifted his blood-soaked shirt. A hole the size of my thumb showed where a bullet had pierced his side.

"This isn't too bad," I said calmly so that Antonio wouldn't be afraid. I looked around. Nearby, a narrow stream of water flowed, and I spotted herbs that might help treat his wound. Antonio turned as I lifted his shirt still farther, and my heart stopped. The bullet's exit had left a ragged and ugly opening the size of my fist.

"Lie down," I said, my voice shaking.

I couldn't rip my tightly woven corte or huipil, so I tore away the bottom of Antonio's shirt and soaked it in the stream. Gently I cleaned his wound, but I knew he needed help I couldn't provide. I rolled some *epazote* in my fingers. The small plant was known to heal cuts, and I hoped it would help Antonio's wound. I placed the epazote into the wound before smearing it over with trementina, the same white pine resin that Papí had burned when he gave his thanks at the caves. At the caves, trementina had helped to heal the soul. Here it covered Antonio's wound, and I prayed it would help protect and heal the body.

Even when covered with trementina, the wound kept oozing blood. I dipped part of my corte into the stream to wipe Antonio's forehead and squeeze water into his mouth. All the while, Alicia watched us, her eyes wide with fear. When Antonio fell into a troubled sleep, I turned to Alicia. "How are you, Ali?" I asked.

Silently she glanced at Antonio and back toward the cantón.

"Did you see Antonio get hurt?" I asked.

Alicia only stared at me.

It was nearly dark, and I knew Antonio couldn't continue, so I forced a smile. "How would you like to stay here tonight, Ali?" I asked.

99

Still Alicia stared quietly.

I left Alicia beside Antonio and climbed a nearby *cereza* tree to gather large black cherries. It had been a long time since I ate, and maybe even longer for my brother and sister. I kept calling to Alicia so she would know I hadn't abandoned her. By the time I finished collecting cherries, Antonio had woken up. It was completely dark, with only a small moon for light. Antonio refused to eat and fell back into another heavy slumber. Alicia ate greedily, but after she finished, she sat and stared at the ground.

"Were the berries good?" I asked her.

Alicia didn't answer. I realized then that she hadn't spoken a single word since I found her naked beneath the bush. Her eyes were distant and preoccupied. I took the hairbrush from my huipil and sat behind Alicia and began to gently brush the mud from her matted and tangled hair. She sat rigid at first, but then slowly she closed her eyes and leaned back against me. I kept stroking the brush through her thick hair.

After Alicia fell asleep, I sat and watched Antonio groaning and shifting in labored sleep. He breathed fast, and when I touched his chest, his heart beat like a drum. I wished desperately that Mamí or Papí could have been there to tell me what to do. Antonio needed help as never before, and I could do nothing. We were too far from any cantón with a curandero to help us, and I wasn't even sure a curandero could help Antonio now.

All we could do was sleep. I unwrapped my corte from my waist and laid it over the three of us like a small blanket. I closed my eyes and felt myself drifting away. I don't know how long I slept before I awoke in the black darkness. Alicia whimpered beside me, hugging her knees and shaking as if the warm night air were cold. Antonio moaned fitfully and finally rolled onto his stomach and pushed himself to his knees with a loud grunt.

"How do you feel?" I asked.

"I hurt so bad," he moaned. "It's like my stomach's on fire."

I could not show my little brother how helpless I felt. Carefully I peeled the trementina from his wound and washed away as much blood as I could. The ground under the wound was matted and soaked with blood. Then I wiped cool water on Antonio's forehead, trying to make up for his weakness with my deliberate movements.

I hadn't wanted to talk of the massacre in front of Alicia, but because she slept now, I asked Antonio, "Can you tell me what happened?"

Antonio gripped his stomach with both hands. "We were working near the cantón when the soldiers came from every direction. Only a few of us escaped. I ran to the trees but heard Alicia screaming behind me. She had been bathing in the stream." Antonio grimaced. "I shouted to her, and that's when I was shot. At first I thought a bee had stung me, but then I saw all the blood. I ran back and carried her to the place where you found us."

I took Antonio's hand and looked at him in the darkness with a great love. This was my brother who had been such a follower. And yet here he lay wounded in the dark from having saved his sister's life. Today he was no follower. "I'm so proud of you," I said. "Mamí and Papí would have been proud, too."

My words seemed to ease Antonio's pain.

Our talking woke Alicia, and she sat up fearfully. I pulled her to my side and hugged her. We had faced hell, but we were still a family.

I tried to stay awake in case Antonio needed comforting. A foul smell came now from his body as he fell in and out of consciousness. He drew in shallow breaths. Sweat dripped from his forehead and pain twisted his face.

I lay awake, listening to the sounds of the forest and to Antonio's moans. Several times I dozed off, waking to the sounds of frogs, crickets, and the breeze. Antonio's labored breath interrupted the harmony of the forest. With each effort he pulled air into his weak body as if through a narrow straw.

Sometime before dawn I dozed off once again. When I awoke next, I heard only the sound of the crickets and nothing more.

Antonio's struggle had ended.

I knelt beside his lifeless body, tears wetting my cheeks. Even in the dark, I saw that the pain had left his face and a calm peacefulness creased his lips. I remained beside Antonio until Alicia awoke, then I held her close.

"Antonio has gone," I said. "Do you understand?"

Alicia stared at Antonio without answering, but her big eyes blinked hard. Finally I stood and removed Antonio's shirt, ripping away the cloth stained by blood at the bottom. I rolled up the sleeves and pulled the ragged shirt over Alicia's small, naked body. The shirt fit her like a dress.

Then I grabbed a stick and dug another shallow hole with hands already blistered from digging other graves. I stabbed angrily at the ground. This wasn't the sacred ground where my brother ought to have been buried. Why was this happening? Everybody was dying, and I was left alive to endure it. Was God mad? Was there something else I could have done to save Antonio's life? That thought haunted me as I rolled my brother into his final resting place.

CHAPTER EIGHT

Morning sun glinted through the trees as Alicia
and I walked away from Antonio's grave. I
refused to look back as we walked north toward the
Mexican border more than two hundred kilometers
away. Such a journey frightened me, but what other
choice did we have? I no longer felt safe in any cantón
or pueblo.

I would rather have waited until dark to walk,
but I was anxious to get away from this place where
Antonio had died. Inside of me I longed to weep and
wake up in Mamí's arms and hear her tell me that
this was only a bad dream, but for Alicia's sake I

forced myself to be strong.

We didn't walk fast, but all day and into the next night we followed narrow walking trails, stopping only to pick cherries, eat roots, and drink water when we crossed streams. Blisters on our feet made us limp, and we stumbled with weariness. Finally, late the next night, Alicia could walk no farther and I found a thick patch of shrubs to sleep under. Our stomachs ached from hunger, but that didn't keep us from sleep.

For the next three days we followed rocky foot trails through the rolling hills, trying to walk mostly at night. We ate only berries and plant roots, and slept during the day. I tried many times to coax words from Alicia, but she refused to speak. Whenever we stopped, she sat as if in a trance while I brushed her hair and hummed familiar songs to her.

We met no one until the fourth day of our journey. Early, before the sun rose, I heard a woman's voice ahead of us crying out weakly in Quiché, "Help! Please, someone help me!"

Thinking that this might be a military trap, I grabbed Alicia and was about to run when I paused to listen more closely.

"Help me. Please!" the female voice called again.

I gripped Alicia's hand tightly and moved forward. There on the ground near the trail, I found a young pregnant woman lying stretched out on top of a corte. Her stomach bulged like a huge melon, and she wore no clothes below her fat waist. Her bare legs and bent knees were spread wide. From where I stood, I heard her heavy breathing and saw her face twisted in pain and dripping sweat.

"Please help," the woman gasped, noticing me. Even as she spoke, she grimaced with pain and held to her round stomach.

"What can I do?" I asked, approaching her and kneeling. "I've never helped anyone give birth before."

"Catch the baby," she cried.

Obediently I kneeled between her legs, but I still wasn't sure what to do. In our cantón, young girls learned many things—to weave, to carry water, to grind corn, to sweep dirt floors, and to make tortillas. We helped our mothers with many chores, but not with birth. That was the job of the midwives, and not even the men were allowed to help.

In our cantón we would hide with other children in nearby bushes while the midwives helped our mothers give birth. We giggled and stared with wide eyes, imagining the terrible things that made our mothers scream and grunt. Sometimes we whispered to each other, guessing what was happening. The boys were mean and said they were killing a pig.

The woman lying in front of me relaxed for a few minutes as if her pain had disappeared, then again she stiffened and grunted and cried out in pain. Desperately I asked, "What hurts?" But the woman couldn't answer.

When the pain left her the next time, the woman said, "Soon. Soon."

I stared. How could a baby be born through such a small opening? Still I waited. Each time the woman stiffened, she screamed louder until I believed she was dying. But finally she screamed, "It's coming! It's coming!"

I looked and saw the baby trying to push out from between her legs. It frightened me. It was like her stomach or intestines coming out. I looked back and saw Alicia watching, her eyes and mouth opened wide. There wasn't time to explain to her what was happening, but I think maybe she thought she was watching another death.

Again the woman grunted and held to her thighs. She strained harder and gasped deeply, as if trying to catch her breath. Sweat dripped from her face in huge drops. The bulge grew larger, like something arriving from a different world. The baby looked like a ball pushing out. Now the woman panted fast. "Catch it," she shouted.

Trembling, I reached out my hands. Suddenly the head of the baby popped out, then one shoulder, and then the next. With each grunt the baby slid farther into my hands. After the chest and stomach squeezed out, I helped pull. Slowly the legs slid from the mother, and suddenly I found myself holding the whole baby, a baby girl. Bloody birth fluids and white paste covered the wrinkled little body, and a long twisted cord ran from between the mother's legs and attached to the baby's stomach.

"What do I do?" I pleaded. "She isn't breathing."

The woman forced her head up and looked. "Clean her mouth with your finger," she grunted.

Afraid the baby was already dead, I ran my finger through its mouth. My finger pulled out thick slime, but still the baby didn't breathe. I wasn't surprised. The baby appeared dead from the beginning, like the dead lambs our sheep aborted in the fields.

"Hold her upside down and hit her backside," the mother grunted.

I lifted the slippery baby up by its ankles, afraid I might drop it. Awkwardly I swatted its back and bottom. Still it hung motionless, but suddenly it gasped and a loud urgent cry pierced the air.

I jumped, nearly dropping the baby. Nervous fear and relief made me laugh. "What now?" I asked.

Again the woman strained to raise her head. "Cut the cord," she whispered, her voice weaker. "And tie a knot, or the baby will bleed to death."

I looked around me. "How do I cut the cord?" I asked.

The mother was too tired to answer me. I looked

around. Alicia sat quietly, watching me with big eyes. I laid the crying baby on the corte between the mother's legs, and then stood. What could I use to cut the cord if I had no machete?

All I could find was some *magüey*, a broad-leaf cactus. I broke off a stiff leaf, careful not to cut myself with the sharp ragged edge, and quickly returned to the mother, who had closed her eyes but still breathed fast like a tired cow.

The baby cried with such a loud voice that I feared soldiers would hear us. Using the jagged magüey leaf, I sliced through the cord. Blood leaked from both cut ends, so I pinched the mother's end while I tried to knot the baby's cord. It was hard, because the cord kept slipping from my shaking fingers, but finally I made a knot and reached down with my mouth to bite onto the bloody end to pull it even tighter.

After I had knotted the mother's cord the same way, I picked up the baby and laid it against the mother's chest. The tired woman opened her eyes and stared weakly but couldn't lift her arms to hold her baby. Her face was pale and she looked ill. The baby still

111

screamed, so I opened the mother's huipil and placed the baby's mouth against the nipple of her swollen breast. The baby wanted to keep crying, but when it felt the nipple against its lips, it caught its breath and began to suck.

I sat beside the exhausted mother and held the uncleaned baby as it nursed. The child was all wrinkled and smeared with blood, birth fluids, and white sticky paste, but still she was beautiful. The magic of what I had witnessed robbed me of my breath. It both frightened and thrilled me. At a time of so much death, new life had been born.

The baby nursed briefly but then cried loudly once again. I forced her mouth back against the mother's swollen breast, but she turned stubbornly away from the nipple and screamed even louder, her piercing wails like a squealing rabbit alerting a hawk. The hawks that I feared wore uniforms and carried guns.

I wanted to ask the mother what I should do with her baby, but she had fallen unconscious. Her breathing was shallow. I glanced fearfully over my shoulder. There across the valley, crossing a sloping field a kilometer away, walked forty or fifty soldiers in uniform, single file. They couldn't hear the baby crying yet, but their trail would soon lead them past the mother, who lay still in the grass as if dead.

I dared not think what soldiers might do to a half-naked woman and a baby. "Soldiers are coming," I whispered loudly, glancing desperately over my shoulder and then back down at the motionless mother. I wanted to panic and hide, but I called Alicia to my side and placed the screaming baby in her arms. "Hold her," I ordered. "I need to hide the mother."

Obediently Alicia held the baby and watched as I grabbed the mother's wrists and dragged her deeper into the trees to where the brush would hide her body from the trail. Alicia followed us, holding the crying baby.

I shook the woman. "What should I do with your baby?" I begged.

The woman's head fell to the side. I shook her again but she refused to wake up. Frantically I looked around. I couldn't just leave the crying baby beside her. The soldiers would soon arrive.

I pulled off the woman's huipil and wrapped it around the baby as a blanket. I spread her dark corte over her to help hide her and to protect her from the mosquitoes and flies that swarmed around us in the morning air. I feared she was dying, but I could do nothing more to help her. There was no water or food to leave with her, and the soldiers walked closer with each second that passed. I needed to escape.

I took the crying infant from Alicia, glanced one last time at the unconscious mother, then rushed into the forest away from the approaching soldiers. I ran as fast as I could, carrying the baby and holding Alicia's hand. In some places I crossed trails but dared not follow them. At times the trees thinned and we were forced to walk out into the open. Those times terrified me. Finally I stopped to catch my breath with the baby still screaming urgently in my arms.

I held the crying baby up to look into its eyes. "Be quiet, little baby!" I said loudly. "I'm trying to save your life. If you want to live, then help me. I'm not your mother, and life isn't always kind."

I knew the baby didn't understand my words, but it

114

hiccuped and stopped crying to look at me. It seemed impossible to me, as I stared at the baby, to think that soldiers had begun their lives so small, vulnerable, and innocent. What was it that corrupted humans so?

I brought the baby gently to my chest and rocked it and quietly sang a song Mamí once sang to me.

> *Hush baby,*
> *Don't cry now.*
> *Birds sing,*
> *Church bells ring.*

> *Hush baby,*
> *Don't be sad.*
> *Never fear.*
> *Mamí's near.*

As I sang, the baby's urgent screams faded into fitful whimpers and she fell asleep on my shoulder. I held my breath; the soldiers could have been anywhere. Slowly I walked, cradling the baby in my arms and humming quietly. Alicia held to my corte and followed me.

The morning sun had climbed high above us, heating the air and bringing thick swarms of mosquitoes. I shooed them from the baby's face. When she woke again, the baby didn't look well. She weighed heavy in my arms, listless and too weak to cry. I walked in circles, tracing my finger gently over the infant's tiny cheeks and wondering what I should do. The baby needed to nurse from its mother, but I doubted the mother still lived, and soldiers most likely surrounded her.

We walked on until we came to a small stream, where I wet the edge of my huipil. Carefully I dripped water into the baby's mouth. She spit the water out and turned her head stubbornly to the side. Again I tried. Finally I lifted the baby and looked into her face again, saying, "Listen to me, little baby. If you love us, you'll live. If you don't, you'll die. Do what you want, but decide quickly, because my sister, Alicia, she needs help, too."

Well, the baby must have loved us. She started sucking on my knuckle and let me squeeze water down my finger into her mouth. Again and again I dipped the edge of my huipil into the stream and squeezed more water until the baby slept once again.

I knew the baby needed more than water to survive, but it was all I had to offer her. I continued walking until the forest opened onto a bare hillside overlooking a big open valley. Spread out below me was a large pueblo I had never seen before. This pueblo was much like the one I had walked to for market. The central plaza looked like the middle of a big nest from the hillside. Surrounding the plaza were a big municipal building, a school, a Catholic church, an outdoor marketplace, and the many *tiendas*, which were small stores containing little more than tables protected by plastic tarps or makeshift wooden roofs. Rows of brown adobe homes spread in every direction, red tile or rusted steel roofing protecting each of them from the weather.

It was market day. People crowded the streets, and the market stalls were piled high with fruit and other goods. Bells rang out from the Catholic Church, announcing the beginning of mass to the many people in the plaza. The sight of the pueblo surprised me.

These people went about life as if there were no danger. Was this pueblo somehow different from our cantón? Alicia cowered and pulled away from me at the sight of the buildings.

I had thought of entering the pueblo with Alicia and the baby, but perhaps that wasn't wise. I was a stranger. If there were soldiers, what would they think of a strange girl entering the pueblo with a scared little girl and a newborn, nearly dead baby? Maybe some soldier would recognize me.

I stood on the hill above the pueblo, my stomach churning with indecision. The baby needed help and so did her mother. Maybe in the market I could find some goat's milk for the baby. She slept too soundly in my arms. I thought of something that Manuel had told me once. He said, "Gabriela, decisions aren't right or wrong when you make them. It's what you do with your decisions that make them right or wrong."

At the edge of the pueblo I decided to leave Alicia alone with the baby for a short time so that I could enter the market. Quickly I would find milk for the baby and help for the mother, then immediately return before the baby woke up.

We walked until only a stand of trees separated us from the nearest homes. I found a thick clump of shrubs for Alicia to hide beneath. "If the baby cries, rock her gently," I told Alicia. "Don't leave this hiding place for any reason."

Alicia refused to answer or nod, but she held the sleeping baby tightly in her arms.

"I'll be right back," I promised. Then I turned and ran into the pueblo.

As I neared the plaza, the sound of music and marimbas filled the air. Papí had always played marimbas, and those familiar sounds flooded my mind with memories. All around me were families, animals, the sounds of children playing, and the smell of cooking. For a moment I wanted to forget everything that had happened. I wanted to begin life over as if no one had died. But even as I daydreamed, I knew Alicia held the sick baby and waited for me.

I rushed across the plaza to the market where I found row after row of vendors bartering their goods. Never had I seen so much food. Carts of colorful fruits and vegetables were piled high near bins bursting with coffee beans, rice, or corn. Fresh meats hung from hooks, and one stand even sold bottled drinks and chocolates. Some vendors sold live animals: chickens, rabbits, goats, and squawking parrots. I headed toward the goats. Back in our cantón I had seen grandmothers feed goat's milk to babies when their mothers fell ill.

As I approached, the vendors stared with surprise at the dirty ghost that walked toward them with tangled hair, a soiled and bloody huipil, and a dirty corte. I knew it was curiosity and not unkindness that made them stare. One vendor motioned for me to come closer.

Hesitantly I approached, and he treated me respectfully, offering me some tortillas and a piece of chicken. Another vendor handed me a bottle of Coca-Cola. I stuffed the food into my mouth and drank faster than a girl should. One man gave me two oranges, and I hid them inside my huipil for Alicia. As I chewed, I explained in Quiché to the man with the goats, "I lost my mother, and my baby sister needs milk." That was the nearest I dared come to the truth.

The man gave me a puzzled look, and when he

120

spoke I realized that he was Ixil and didn't speak Quiché. Hesitantly, I spoke a little Spanish, but he didn't understand that either, so I pointed to a small gourd he had filled with milk. He hesitated, but then handed me the milk with a kind smile. I nodded my thanks and carried the gourd carefully back across the plaza.

Still I trusted no one. Suddenly a soft touch on my shoulder made me jump. I turned to find an old nun looking at me. Deep wrinkles creased the woman's face. Her skin was shriveled like a dried orange, and her shoulders sagged as if under some invisible load. She smiled at me, her squinting eyes glowing with curiosity and kindness. "Hello, I'm Mother Lopez," she said in Spanish.

I had seen soldiers dress as priests, but never as nuns. No soldier could have faked such a look of kindness. Cautiously I spoke in Spanish. "My name is Gabriela," I said.

"You speak Spanish well for an India," the nun said.

"You must help me," I said. "This morning my little sister and I found a mother giving birth alone in the countryside. I helped her, but then because there were soldiers nearby, I had to hide the mother and we brought the baby here. My little sister is outside the pueblo, hiding with the baby."

The nun nodded. "Show me where they are."

As the nun began to follow me, gunshots echoed loudly in the air. Then we heard screaming and looked around. From the narrow side streets, soldiers suddenly appeared, firing their rifles into the air and herding people toward the center of the plaza. As we watched, an Ixil husband and wife ignored the soldier's commands and ran past them, trying to escape. Two soldiers aimed their rifles and fired. The couple stumbled and then fell lifeless to the ground, their bodies suddenly still.

"Come with me," the nun shouted, grabbing my hand and spilling the gourd of milk on the ground. "Let's go to the church."

"I must go to my sister," I shouted back, twisting my hand free and running back down an empty alley.

Suddenly more soldiers appeared ahead of me, firing their rifles recklessly as they came. I wanted only to escape, so I returned to the plaza and ran in a different direction, but the soldiers were everywhere, completely surrounding us.

Without thinking, I ran across the plaza to a single large machichi tree thick with branches and leaves. I ignored all that happened around me as I reached up and began climbing.

Below me, people ran in every direction like scared cattle. Soldiers surrounded everyone. I climbed faster. In a forest it was easy to hide in a tree surrounded by other trees, but the machichi tree in the plaza stood alone, a single tree surrounded by buildings, streets, frightened people, and dangerous soldiers. When I reached the upper branches, I peeked down through the thick leaves and saw soldiers. They shouted and cursed and fired their rifles as they herded the terrified people. I feared that some of the bullets they fired recklessly into the air might hit me.

Soon the ugly and dangerous men surrounded not only the people of the pueblo but also the tree I had climbed. I, too, was a prisoner.

CHAPTER NINE

Fear froze my muscles. With soldiers less than ten meters below me, it was as if a big fist pinched my throat and squeezed the air from my chest. The soldiers could have seen me through the leaves of the machichi tree if they had looked straight up, but they were too busy shouting and waving their rifles at the scared people who churned frantically about the plaza.

I peeked out from between the leaves at the vendors across the plaza who tried to hide, crouching behind their stands. The soldiers spotted them and opened fire. From my tree I watched men and women falling dead across their stands, spilling fruit, coffee, and vegetables onto the dirt. Goats and sheep bawled and twisted frantically at the ends of their tethers.

Many people ran toward the church near the tree where I hid. Inside, a priest called loudly for everyone to be quiet and not to be afraid. "This is a place of God," he shouted. "God will care for us. If the soldiers hurt us here, we'll all go to Heaven together."

I don't think God heard our prayers that day. A small band of soldiers burst into the church. Muffled shots quieted the priest's voice, then people from the church spilled out through the large double doors, only to be met by other soldiers who herded them like cattle across the plaza, where all the other villagers waited. I spotted Mother Lopez among them.

The soldiers shoved everybody into the center of the plaza and separated them. They shouted loudly, "All men—into the church! Leave your knives and machetes outside by the tree. All women go to the municipal building. Children, go to the schoolhouse."

"We're taking a census," shouted one soldier. "This is only for administrative purposes."

I wanted to scream down from the tree, "Don't

believe them! They lie!" But I dared not move or make a sound.

Most obeyed the soldiers quickly, fear glistening in their eyes, but a few of the men refused to leave their families. The soldiers approached those men, clubbed them down with the butts of their rifles, and dragged them unconscious or struggling into the church. After three men were clubbed down, the rest left their wives and children without argument.

Some children clung to their mothers and were forcefully pulled away and dragged screaming into the schoolhouse with the rest. One mother held desperately to her baby, but the swing of a rifle broke her arm and a soldier carried her crying baby away, upside down by a single leg.

When the plaza had been cleared of all campesinos and Indios, guards positioned themselves outside each building. Other soldiers brought wood from people's homes and built a big fire in the plaza. I didn't understand at first why they had started such a big fire on a warm day. They separated themselves into three groups. Some soldiers went to the schoolhouse, some to the church, and some to the municipal building. These men joined guards who were already stationed outside each structure.

The goats and sheep kept bawling and twisting against their ropes, trying to escape. Dogs cowered in corners and against walls. The soldiers laughed and shot the animals one at a time, as if for practice. When that shooting ended and every creature lay dead, all was quiet for a few minutes. The only sounds I heard came from the church, where men pleaded to be released and returned to their families. But soon their begging turned to cries of fear, and before long, terrible screams of pain echoed from inside the church. I covered my ears, but nothing could mute the sounds of torture.

I imagined these same sounds echoing through my own cantón when my family was killed. I thought also of Alicia and the baby. Could they hear this shooting? I had promised Papí that I would care for our family, but I had failed everyone, even Alicia. It hurt to imagine her totally alone under the bush, frightened, holding a sick baby and depending on my return.

A new kind of scream made me look toward the municipal building, where all the women had been taken. The soldiers had dragged a young woman outside. They shoved her into the plaza, ripping off her corte, her huipil, and then her undergarments. She fought and struggled, but the soldiers held her naked. She bit one of them, and he slapped her so hard that even from up in the tree I saw blood flow from her mouth. I will never forget how the soldiers laughed as they lined up and waited their turn to rape that woman.

It was terrifying to watch what that woman endured. She was so brave. Never once did she scream or cry out from the pain as each new soldier pummeled her on the ground. Some soldiers struck her as they raped her. Her only escape was to close her eyes and turn her head away from the animals who grunted and laughed as they violated her body and her dignity.

Louder than the soldiers' sadistic laughs were the screams of torture echoing from inside the church. The screams would grow louder and louder, then suddenly fall quiet. Then the door of the church opened again and soldiers dragged another body out across the plaza and dumped it onto the flames. The corpses were bloody, with ears and noses and fingers missing.

I felt relief when the last soldier finished raping the woman. Maybe now she would be released or allowed to return to the other women. Instead, a soldier walked up to her as casually as if he were lighting his cigarette. He pulled out his pistol. I looked quickly away as a loud shot echoed up from the plaza. When I peeked again, two soldiers had dragged her body to the fire.

My body trembled as if the tree were shaking. Tears blurred my vision, and I swallowed back desperate screams. I needed to throw up but didn't dare. For many long minutes I clung to the branches, gasping with anger and fear. At least the woman's suffering had ended. This was the same relief I had felt the day Manuel died from his beating.

Immediately another woman was led struggling from the building and the raping continued, as soldiers argued with each other to go first. For hours I watched from the machichi tree as bodies were thrown into the flames. Soldiers used their knives to pry gold-filled teeth from the corpses before they were dumped into the hungry fire.

I wanted desperately to close my eyes, but I feared being spotted or falling. I tried instead to cover my ears, but I couldn't block out the desperate screams and cries of pain. Many different Mayan languages filled the air with screams and cries that day, but the laughter and joking of the soldiers knew only one language. Spanish.

Before dark, a small number of soldiers gathered under the machichi tree to eat and take short siestas in the shade. I froze like a shadow. If even one soldier glanced up he would spot me. I stared at the bark of the tree and at my skin and at the sky, trying desperately to stay still until the soldiers under the tree woke and returned to their evil.

For the first time I realized how hungry I had become. I had no choice but to ignore my grumbling stomach, but the atrocities that continued in the plaza could not be so easily ignored. Again and again my breath caught in my throat and a bitter taste built in my mouth. I kept swallowing to keep from throwing up. Finally I closed my eyes.

When I opened my eyes again, the sun had set. I hoped that with the coming of night the soldiers would finally grow tired and stop their insanity. Instead, they began drinking and their actions only grew more violent. The darkness kept me from seeing across the plaza, but desperate bloody screams pierced the night and told me that the evil continued.

During the night, soldiers took turns sleeping under the tree, so close to me that I heard their vulgar talk and listened to their snoring. I had thought the soldiers were animals, but not even animals could have slept through such screams. I pinched my eyes closed again, pretending that the screaming was only monkeys and that the echo of gunfire was only thunder. I tried to imagine flowers and sunsets, but beauty was too far away at that moment to be imagined.

I grew nauseated from weariness, and when the killing continued, I feared growing so tired that I might fall from the tree. I had walked all of the previous night and had not slept all day. I also needed to urinate, but I didn't dare.

The screaming kept me awake late into the night. Sometimes I stared up at the sky for long periods, watching the clouds make ghostly images as they passed over the moon. The stars looked like bullet holes shot into Heaven. Soon my need to urinate became a desperate thing. Finally, with soldiers sleeping barely twenty feet below me, I silently relieved myself, letting my undergarments and corte absorb the fluid.

By now my legs had gone completely numb and I feared falling. Carefully I squirmed and twisted my body, trying to bring back circulation to my limbs. I dared not swing my arms or kick my legs. All through the night I suffered my own silent torture until the sky finally grew light with the coming of dawn. At sunrise, not one rooster crowed.

The coming of morning brought new horrors. Children were brought out from the schoolhouse to watch their parents being tortured and raped. And throughout the atrocities, the sadistic evil laughter of the soldiers echoed among the buildings and up through the branches of the tree.

A helicopter flew over and circled the pueblo, and soldiers looked up and waved, then returned to their killing. I pulled branches over my head, hoping the helicopter wouldn't spot me.

Later that morning, several soldiers took a group of children and marched them around the plaza with sticks on their shoulders like soldiers carrying guns. All of the children cried with fright. The soldiers shouted at them, "Turn right! Turn left! Stop!" When a child stopped too soon or turned wrong, that child was pulled from the formation and punished. I had to turn my eyes away. By the time they finished, every child had been pulled from the formation. None survived.

I actually wondered if maybe the cruel things I was seeing were only a part of a bad dream, part of my own imagination and insanity. Surely humans could not be so cruel. But this nightmare was not a dream from which I could awaken.

When at last the only females left were old and wrinkled grandmothers, the soldiers grew angry and led the remaining few out into the plaza and stripped them naked. Mother Lopez was among these women, but the soldiers treated her with no deference. At gunpoint the grandmothers were ordered to perform like circus animals.

Most of the old women, including Mother Lopez, had so much dignity that they refused to do what was commanded and instead kneeled quietly on the ground to accept their fate. Angry cursing and threats sounded from the soldiers. When the old women still remained kneeling, loud gunshots left their fragile and aged bodies crumpled on the ground.

My body pained me from sitting motionless on the branch, and at one point I nearly crawled from the tree and surrendered to the soldiers. I wanted to join those sparks from the fire that floated upward. After all I had seen, what reason was there to continue living? But my anger burned as hot as the flames in the plaza. My revenge would be to stay alive and someday speak of what I witnessed.

My body and mind had become so weary by this time that even with the madness below me, my head nodded and I jerked awake again and again to catch myself from falling. I ached so badly that I nearly cried out. Once more I urinated into my clothes. My grip on the branches was so weak now, I couldn't have lifted a broom. I could barely even swallow.

The pile of burning bodies made a small hill in the plaza, and a wretched scorched smell filled the air. Those devils would have kept killing if there had been a thousand people, but by late afternoon every living human and creature had been murdered except me. The soldiers gathered in the center of the plaza, dirt and blood smearing their wrinkled and torn uniforms. Their unshaven faces made them look like beggars and bandits.

The men went to the *pilas*, the big washing sinks near the church where women washed their clothes. They shaved their faces and took turns washing the blood from their uniforms and skin so that they could return home clean to their own wives and children. I knew that their souls could not be so easily cleaned. After what had happened, I hoped they were all damned to hell.

Before leaving the pueblo, the soldiers spread out in different directions, carrying torches and setting fire to every structure. Within an hour, all of the pueblo blazed with rumbling flames. Even in the tree, heat forced me to pull my huipil over my face. I feared that the branches and leaves might catch fire.

With flames surrounding me, the pueblo became a literal hell of raging fires as the soldiers returned to the plaza carrying their rifles. Their packs bulged with stolen money and jewelry. At last, late in the afternoon, the soldiers walked single file away from the burning pueblo as calmly as if they had just finished another ordinary day of work.

By this time, I had lost all hope. I feared climbing from the tree, but I had no choice. My body was so weak and my mind so numb. My muscles ached and felt frozen as I began working my way down. Inch by inch I crawled from a tree that had taken only seconds to climb the day before. I used my arms to hold on to the branches because my hands were too weak. My legs threatened to collapse with each movement.

Ten feet above the ground, my body simply gave out and I slipped, crashing from the tree and landing hard on my side, knocking the air from my lungs. I lay there dazed, gasping for breath, and trying to decide if anything was broken. I stared back up into the tree where I'd spent the last two days and was overcome with guilt for having survived. I deserved to die along with everyone else.

Climbing that tree had not been an act of bravery. It was the act of a desperate coward. Everyone else had faced the soldiers except me. I had hidden while others died. By being a Tree Girl, I had been a coward.

There was a time when trees brought me closer to Heaven, but climbing the tree in the plaza had brought me closer to Hell. I made a promise to myself that day. As I lay exhausted and nearly unconscious beneath the machichi tree in the middle of that burning pueblo, with smoke clouding the air and the wretched smell of burned bodies as thick as the haze around me, I made a solemn vow to the earth and to the sky and to everything left sacred in the world: Never again would I climb a tree.

CHAPTER TEN

As I lay under the machichi tree, my conscience screamed at me, *Gabriela, get up and leave now! Go to where you left Alicia and the baby!*

I tried to stand but couldn't. I was dizzy and weak. My dry and swollen tongue filled my mouth and threatened to suffocate me, and every part of my body hurt. I lay moaning on the ground, exhausted, needing water, but first my body demanded a few moments of rest.

Finally I struggled to my feet, stumbling like a drunken man across the plaza and into the marketplace. Little remained from the massacre except spilled fruit, charred ashes from the vendors' stands, dark bloodstains in the dirt, and everywhere the stinking carcasses of rotting animals. Much of the bread that remained had hardened. Meat brought fresh to market had rotted, the odor mingling with the stench of death.

I picked my way among the destruction until I found an old clay jug full of stale water. I gulped mouthful after mouthful of the warm foul liquid until my thirst was satisfied. Then I picked my way through the destroyed stands, eating a piece of fruit, an old chunk of salted meat, a dried cookie, and anything else I could find. I wrapped my waist strap tightly around my corte and filled the front of my huipil with whatever I didn't eat.

I made my way toward the edge of the pueblo to search for Alicia and the baby. I kept looking over my shoulder, expecting more soldiers to appear at any moment. I tried to run but couldn't. I was still weak, and my legs threatened to collapse under me.

At the place where I had left my little sister, I called out and crawled behind the bush. Alicia and the baby were gone. Frantically I looked in every direction, searching for tracks in the hardened earth and imagining the worst. What if the soldiers had found Alicia and taken her and the baby to the schoolhouse in the pueblo? I dared not allow such a thought.

The unnatural stillness of the air hung heavy with danger. I continued searching farther and farther out into the countryside, thinking maybe Alicia had run with the baby. Behind me in the distance, thick smoke still rose into the sky from the fires in the pueblo. The afternoon air cooled, but I refused to give up.

When darkness finally blanketed the countryside, I finally sank to the ground in tears. Every living human I had ever known was gone. There on the hard ground in the dark, severed from all that I had ever known and loved, I sobbed uncontrollably. Memories of my family and friends and my past haunted me.

For a long time I lay motionless on the ground and waited for my soul to join the sparks that had drifted to the heavens back in the pueblo. That was where I should have died. Now I wanted everything to end—my loss, the pain, my memories, my life. But a dog barked and barked in the distance. The moon still hung above me in the sky, and around me the sounds of crickets chorused. I still breathed, and life refused to end so easily.

Finally, I forced myself to stand. I looked back toward the pueblo at the dull glow of flames still tinting the sky, then I turned and wandered toward the North Star. What else could I do? My heart still beat, and tonight life wouldn't surrender and allow me to quit. For two full nights I'd been without sleep, but still I stumbled blindly into the next night, moving forward in a drunken stupor until at last my body would go no farther.

I didn't search for soft or protected ground to sleep. I simply quit walking and collapsed, unconscious before my body met the earth. The sleep of the dead captured me, not allowing me to wake either for the heavy rain that came during the night or for the coming of dawn. Only when the sun climbed high in the sky and made the air hot around me—only then did I roll onto my stomach and open my eyes.

I found my clothes and hair soaked from the downpour, and I coughed and stared around me at the wet ground. I still lived, whatever that meant. Struggling to my feet, I continued northward.

The first days after the massacre, I must have been in shock. I remember little of that time except walking, sleeping, and weeping. Always I wept as I walked, each day surrounded by lonely winds, hot days, long cold nights, crickets chirping, and the crying of doves. I remember hearing doves.

I ate sparingly from the food I carried, and when my path crossed a stream or a spring, I soaked some of my dry bread to make it easier to swallow. I didn't choose to be alive. I ate because as long as I still lived, I felt hunger.

I tried to avoid people by keeping to trails high on the hills, but many of those who escaped the killings in other cantóns and pueblos also walked the same trails northward. Whenever someone came near, I hid in the trees or ran.

One afternoon I was walking sullenly, staring at my feet, when a voice surprised me from behind. I turned to find myself only a few feet away from a family of Indios who had walked up behind me. A mother, father, grandmother, and one little child stared at me. I started to run, but I saw in their faces the same haunted desperation I also felt. These people were no threat to me. I stared back at them briefly, neither of us greeting the other, and then I continued on alone.

With the passing of each day, more Indios found their way to the trails—mothers, fathers, grandparents, and children. Like me, most had only the clothes they wore and the heavy loss they carried in their hearts. Many limped and nursed wounds. Others threw up and sweated from illness. Each day heat came like an oven, and each night brought bitter cold. Many parents and grandparents trudged along carrying sick children on their backs. I isolated myself from everybody, carrying on my back the burden of shame for having survived when so many others had had the courage to die.

Where could so many people have come from? There were hundreds, many of whom wore the clothes and spoke the language of other regions. Everybody, however, shared the same vacant expression of despair.

One day, as I ate from the food I carried, two old men approached me with their hands held out begging. I shook my head and ran from them. Another day, an old woman approached me searching for a lost family member. Again I shook my head. My responsibility had been a family that now lay buried. My only responsibility now was feeding myself and searching for a young girl named Alicia and a baby I had never wanted.

Some days, platoons of soldiers passed on distant hillsides and gunshots echoed in the distance. Rumors of ambushes spread among the refugees. For this reason, most refugees walked during the night, which was hard because of the cold and the twisting rocky trails. Some nights, heavy clouds hid the moon and made traveling even more dangerous, but never as dangerous as a soldier's gun.

There were some who risked walking during the day, but I didn't. I hid among the trees or in caves or behind large boulders until nightfall, avoiding everyone, especially those who started fires or had children who made noise. When I finished the food carried with me from the pueblo, I spent my days as the others did, sleeping or picking berries, *jocote* fruit, or digging for raw *pacaya*, a bitter-tasting root that Mamí and Papí had taught me to eat. My nights and days were consumed with overwhelming anger and guilt.

Sometimes when I walked close to a group, I over-heard their stories. Men showed their wounds and told of being caught and tortured. Most of the women remained silent, not willing to share the memories they guarded. All of the refugees spoke of losing family or friends to the war.

I walked alone, but remained close to one large group. I never knew where I was as we journeyed northward. I knew only that I walked each day closer to a frightening and unknown fate. Some days, in the far northern hills of Guatemala, we passed small can-tóns filled with mostly Indios. I didn't dare enter those places for fear soldiers might be waiting in ambush. I knew also that the villagers in those cantóns were very poor and probably didn't have enough food to feed their own families.

Sometimes strangers approached the refugees, offering directions or telling them where soldiers had been. Always I feared these people were setting mili-tary traps. I worried that if we believed them, we might die, but if we didn't believe them, we might still die.

Everyone lived in constant fear of dying, never trusting anybody.

Rumors of more killings to the south continued, but after many nights of travel without hearing gunshots and many days without seeing patrols, I decided I must be north of where the soldiers destroyed cantóns and killed the Indios. Still fearful and cautious, I began walking in daylight. This was easier, but I noticed that everybody who owned a machete carried it always at their side. I carried a big stick. Every voice, every breaking branch in the forest, even the sound of a hawk's cry made me look around, certain that the soldiers had caught up with me.

Food grew scarce to the north. I spent whole days searching for enough food for one small meal. More and more people begged from me, but I turned and walked away from them. I feared people and wanted nothing from them, nor did I wish to give anything of myself. I existed in an isolated world of memories, anger, and hurt.

Sometimes I glanced at the children on the trail and felt twinges of pity when I saw their small faces so haunted by fear and hunger. Their faces brought back painful memories of another place that had children with names like Antonio, Rubén, Victoria, Lidia, Lisa, Pablo, Federico, Lester, and Alicia. But I reminded myself that the children on the trail weren't my responsibility either. I searched for the only responsibilities I had, Alicia and the baby. But each day I lost a little more hope.

As my journey took me farther north, refugees stretched down the trails for many kilometers, streams of humankind fleeing death. We were a mass of thousands, but still we walked in smaller distinguishable groups. I remained with one particular group of Indios for no reason except that they had become familiar. I no longer distrusted their faces or mistook them for soldiers sent to spy on us. Still I spoke to nobody, helped nobody, and asked for nothing. Sometimes I walked ahead of our group to search for Alicia and the baby, never really expecting to find them. Each passing week, my hope faded.

One afternoon our group walked past a large cereza

tree filled with soft black cherries. The others who walked with me were old and couldn't climb trees. I knew that I could easily climb and gather cherries for everyone, but I also knew I had promised myself I'd never again climb a tree. The memories from the pueblo were raw in my mind.

"Will you climb the tree and gather cherries for us?" the old people asked me.

My heart beat faster and I shook my head, angered by their accusing stares of disappointment. When they asked again, I ran from the group and walked alone the rest of the day. Climbing trees had brought me enough pain.

The passing of each day found the refugees farther from the danger of soldiers, but new enemies arrived, bringing death with them. Starvation, diarrhea, cholera, measles, fever, vomiting, amoebas, and malnutrition—they killed each day as surely as any bullet. It became harder to ignore the children I saw, their arms and legs growing thinner and their bellies bulging more each day from starvation. When I was growing up, my parents taught me the healing power of the herbs and plants of the forest. My brothers, my sisters, and I had known that we could always find food and medicine if the crops failed. This knowledge was a gift from my parents. But now I ignored that gift and told myself again and again that these children weren't my responsibility.

As for me, I had lost much weight. I passed a pile of garbage one day and spotted a small piece of broken mirror. When I stared at my own reflection, my cheeks hollow, my eyes sunken, I looked like someone from the grave. My hair, which I normally kept brushed, had grown matted and tangled. Even though I still carried the brush in my huipil, brushing my hair wasn't important anymore. Surviving was all I knew.

Because of the starvation and the diseases, every few kilometers refugees could be seen burying their friends or family members beside the trails. Sometimes the ground was too hard or rocky and stones were piled over a body. Sometimes a body lay abandoned and ignored, flies thick around the face. By the time I neared the Mexican border, I feared that many more people were close to dying, but I ignored the deaths.

150

Anybody who depended on me would end up no bet-ter off than my brothers and sisters had.

One afternoon, some of the refugees near me spoke intensely. "Ahead thirty kilometers is the border," one said. "We don't know if the border officials will let us cross, but if they do, soon we'll come to a refugee camp where we'll be safe. We've been told that the Mexican officials at the camp won't force us to return to Guatemala."

I didn't know if I could trust what the man said. Walking thirty kilometers seemed so far, but I had to keep going or starve. I pitied the old people. Many would never make it another thirty kilometers. They were simply living out the last hours of their lives with empty hope.

Five more days passed before I reached the Mexican border. The group I traveled with had slowed so much that I left them behind and traveled alone the last two days. I knew many in that small group needed help des-perately, but I couldn't help their suffering.

As I neared the border, I met refugees returning

who said they had been turned back by border guards. Now I wasn't sure what to do. The moon at that time was barely a sliver, making it treacherous walking in the blackness of the night, but near the border, trees were scarce. There was no choice but to try to cross at night with only darkness to hide my crossing.

I ate all I could find during the day, and then walked through a long night, skirting the border crossing by a full kilometer. I came to a large river and had no choice but to wade across. In the middle, the water reached my chest and the current pulled at my body. This terrified me because I couldn't swim very well, but finally I reached the far side.

I waited until dawn to double back to the road, moving cautiously, testing each step. As the sun rose the next morning, I reached the road I thought might lead me to the refugee camp. I no longer saw other refugees and hoped it was because I had made it across the border into Mexico.

It frightened me to walk near the road where there was no protection, but all day I walked on, seeing only a few buses pass. Late that afternoon, I spotted the camp in the distance. I was weary and glad to have reached the end of a long journey. As I neared the camp, the dusty air carried the sounds of babies crying. Ahead, hundreds of refugees crowded the small encampment. Slabs of wood or plastic were their only shelter. They sat around in small groups, watching me, their stares indifferent.

Two Mexican officials met me as I approached. Their uniforms and rifles made me want to run. The officers shook their heads as they stopped me. They spoke in Spanish. "This camp is full. Keep going to the camp near San Miguel."

"How far is that?" I asked, hesitantly replying in Spanish.

The official pointed. "Another thirty kilometers ahead."

I nearly cried. "Please," I said. "Someone said I could stay here."

The official's scowl left no room for argument. "We're full," he growled.

CHAPTER ELEVEN

It took me only three days to reach the San Miguel refugee camp, because on the last afternoon a family in a pickup truck stopped and offered me a ride for the final ten kilometers. At first I shook my head at the driver, but he traveled with his wife and children. I was weary and hungry, and I reasoned that soldiers wouldn't travel with their families. Still I worried. Maybe the driver would take me back to the border crossing and turn me in. I no longer trusted anyone. I sat in the open back of the truck, tense, ready to jump. Even from a moving pickup.

The man who drove did as he had offered and let

me off beside the highway near San Miguel. He pointed to the refugee camp one kilometer away down a rutted dirt road. I walked the last kilometer, my apprehension building with each step. What if they turned me away from this place?

Nothing could have prepared me for the San Miguel refugee camp. Instead of a camp with tents or some other kind of shelter for maybe six or seven hundred people, I found thousands of refugees whose shelters and belongings looked like fields of garbage—rusted sheets of tin, ragged pieces of blankets, cardboard, old boards, plastic held up by sticks or anything else that might help to ward off the hot sun, the cold nights, or winds and rain. The camp stretched as far as I could see among the rocks and brush.

Hesitantly I ventured among the scattered people who wandered about, their clothes hanging from their thin bodies like rags on skeletons. Nobody spoke to me. A few people watched me idly, but to most I seemed not to exist. I was one of them, my body gaunt, my hair and my clothes matted and dirty, smelling of waste.

Ahead, a group of refugees massed. When I approached, I found a parked tanker truck with long lines of refugees waiting their turn to fill plastic containers with water. Most of the containers were bright red and blue, and they must have only recently been given to the refugees, because nothing else in their world was new.

Beyond the water truck, another crowd gathered. Two white, *gringo* aid workers shouted and pushed, handing out food from another truck, struggling to divide their load among the shoving crowds. One held up a small bag of rice and yelled in Spanish, "This must last your family for two weeks!"

I couldn't believe how the refugees acted. They were like animals chasing scraps. With each new bag the aid worker lifted above his head, the group surged forward, yelling, pushing, and shoving. "Back up!" he screamed, but I doubted many of the refugees understood his Spanish. I watched several bags being torn open and spilled on the ground by those fighting over them.

I refused to be a part of such madness, so I kept

wandering the camp. As I walked, I searched for Alicia. The journey to the camp had been long and hard, and it seemed unlikely that Alicia would have completed it before me. I knew that it was unlikely that she would complete such a journey in one week, one year, or even one lifetime. Still, I refused to accept that she had been killed. I refused to allow the thought that maybe Alicia and the baby had been found and taken to the schoolhouse in the pueblo. To avoid that thought alone, I would keep looking for the rest of my life. Always I would search for a little girl with long black hair and a stubborn chin, a special little girl who would turn and answer when I called, "Alicia!"

As I walked deeper into the camp, I could find no place for people to wash or clean themselves. To go to the bathroom, I had to stand exposed beside everybody else along a public ditch. The more I explored, the more it seemed that the refugees had grouped themselves roughly by language. I found one section of camp where most spoke Quiché, but nobody offered me help. Finding shelter or food was up to me. Realizing this, I turned and headed back toward the trucks.

All afternoon and evening I crowded with others around the trucks, but only those who pushed or fought the hardest could get any of the supplies. By nightfall, I still had no food or shelter. At last I curled up on open ground under a tattered old piece of cardboard that did little to keep me warm. This camp, like our cantón back home, sat high in the mountains. Some nights the cold air formed thin ice on the mud puddles. That first night I shivered and clenched my teeth, hugging my knees and breathing inside my huipil. I slept little.

When dawn came, my stomach knotted with hunger and I needed water. The morning air hung heavy like a cloud, thick with dust and smoke and the smell of human waste. Hungry babies cried, and everywhere children coughed continuously. Yawning hard, I stood and went directly to the water truck. Already a long line had formed, but I noticed that the faucet splashed as people filled their jugs. Some of the water dripped down the side of the truck onto the ground.

I ignored loud swearing from those in line as I crawled under the truck. Carefully I positioned my head so that the water dripped into my mouth. When those in line realized I was not trying to take a place in line ahead of them, they ignored me. For a long time I lay there, letting water drip into my mouth. Finally I stood and went in search of food and something to use for shelter.

I found one big truck that handed out donated clothes. The aid workers rolled items into balls and threw them randomly. I needed to find something to protect myself from the cold, so I elbowed in among the others. After pushing and being pushed for most of the afternoon, I finally caught a sweater.

I retreated back from the shoving mass of people and tried it on. I think it could have fit a horse. The waist hung to the ground like a dress, and the sleeves had to be rolled up to free my hands. I couldn't imagine any person big enough to need such a sweater, but I didn't care. It was all I had to keep me warm that night.

Others also tried on the clothes they caught. One woman pulled on pants that were so thin and tight they made her skin look black. She looked around in embarrassment, greatly disappointed that this was her reward for a hot afternoon of shoving and pushing in the sun.

Some were lucky and found themselves with heavy blankets and jackets. Others caught only fancy shirts or blouses. These would have looked good at a dance, but there were no dances at the refugee camp. One old grandmother pulled on a big leather vest that looked like armor on her thin, bony frame. She examined it with a look of wonderment, and then flashed a big toothless grin at the rest of us and walked proudly in circles. We all laughed. I realized it was my first laughter in more than two months.

I rolled up the sweater and held it tightly in my arms as I went in search of food. I had grown weak from not eating. All of that afternoon and into the night I looked. Anywhere a truck stopped, crowds gathered instantly. Even late at night, refugees wandered around the camp hoping to find scraps of food.

It was late that night before I collected a small loaf of bread and some hot soup handed out by an American woman in a van. I also collected a handful of rice and enough corn flour to make a few tortillas if I could find a way to cook. I went again to the tanker truck and caught water with my mouth. Still I had no way of carrying anything, but tomorrow I would try to find a jug.

That night I slept better, but the camp woke early. By sunrise I was up trading some of my food to a woman who had a pan and made tortillas for me from the flour I had found. Then I again wandered the camp, putting every morsel of food I found into my mouth. There were no mealtimes, only constant scavenging, and I threw nothing away. I traded a pair of men's pants I collected for a water jug that leaked. I also found a small piece of black plastic, which I wrapped around me during the next several nights. That, along with the big sweater, helped to ward off the night cold, but still I needed a shelter for the sun and rain.

Always while I scavenged, I looked for Alicia, turning at the sound of every child's yell.

By the end of the first week, I had become like all of the rest who crowded the aid workers, my arms pushing and reaching, my voice pleading. I, too, behaved like an animal, kicking and shoving others to capture anything thrown to us. I hated living and behaving this way. This wasn't how my parents had raised me, but starvation was the only alternative.

Ten days after I first arrived, I approached a truck handing out supplies. Because blankets and plastic tarps were being distributed, the crowd was frenzied and pushing hard. Fights broke out as a dozen people grabbed for each item pitched randomly into the desperate crowd. I watched for a few minutes, but then realized the truck would be empty soon. I still had nothing to serve as my shelter.

I had no choice. Pushing and shoving, I squirmed my way closer to the truck. If someone bigger pushed me, I stepped on their toes as if by accident. One man slapped me. I waited until a package with a blue plastic tarp landed near me, and I dove on it and fought like a cat against a swarm of other bodies, pulling and yanking and kicking. Once I got ahold of the package, I held to it tightly. Two old ladies and a young teenage boy also refused to let go of the package, so I shoved hard and all of them sprawled to the ground. I grabbed the tarp from them and gripped it as I turned and ran.

The refugees I pushed over gave up and turned back to the truck for their next opportunity. I retreated to an open stretch of ground to hide the tarp inside my huipil. This blue tarp was large enough to make a rough tent or lean-to. Finally I had a shelter. As I stood admiring the tarp, I glanced up and noticed the two old ladies I had pushed. Together they walked from the crowd, one limping badly and the other helping her. Both wept.

In that moment a sudden shame swept over me. Those grandmothers needed the tarp even more desperately than I did. Would they now have to sleep cold tonight? Would tomorrow find them dead in the hot sun without shade? All because of me. What had I become? Was my dignity only as deep as the dirt on my skin? Was my pride worth only as much as a plastic tarp? If so, then why should I even survive? Mamí and Papí would have been so ashamed of me at that moment.

I ran after the old women and called to them in

Spanish, "Here, this is yours." I held out the tarp.

The women turned, and for a moment fear clouded their faces.

"Please, don't be afraid," I said.

"That tarp is yours," answered the woman who had been limping. "Don't tease us."

I shook my head. "I'm not teasing you." I placed the tarp in the lady's arms. "What I did was wrong. Please take it."

Surprised, the woman held up the package and looked at it. "What will you use?" she asked.

I shook my head. "Maybe I can find another one."

"Do you have a family here?" demanded the other woman loudly. Her body was as thin as a skeleton.

I shook my head.

The woman reached and took the package. She pulled the plastic and spread it out on the ground. I stood watching, not sure what she was doing as she twisted the tarp this way and that. Then, as if her mind was made up, she turned to me and announced, "It's big enough for all three of us. Go find some pieces of wood to hold it up."

"But I don't want to bother—"

The woman placed her skinny hand across my mouth. "Don't talk so much. Life is hard enough. Go get some wood before I give you a spanking."

That was how I first met Rosa and Carmen, two *Kakchikel* women. They hadn't known each other before arriving at the camp. They should have been playing with grandchildren in a cantón somewhere, but life had decided differently.

"Do you know where you want to place the tarp?" I asked.

Rosa, the skinny one, laughed loudly. "It doesn't matter. We can put it on the beach by the lake." She spread her arm widely. "Or we can put it in the grass by the river. It doesn't matter."

Carmen shrugged. "We don't have anyplace yet."

"Come with me," I said, taking Carmen's arm to help her. "Did I hurt you?" I asked.

Carmen smiled. "Yes, you pushed hard."

"I bite, too," I said, which made them both laugh. Because I didn't know any others who spoke Kakchikel, I took them to where I had slept among the

Quiché. "You two stay here. I'll bring some wood to put up the tarp."

Rosa and Carmen looked at me like two old mothers. "You come back quickly or you won't get hot tamales and enchiladas for supper," Rosa threatened.

"What about ice cream?" I asked.

"No ice cream," Rosa said, bursting into another fit of laughter. "That's because you pushed Carmen."

"I'll be back," I promised.

Around me were many shrubs, but none large enough to hold up the front and back of the tarp like a tent. I walked quickly to the edge of the camp, looking for bigger branches and pieces of wood. On a small rise a kilometer from camp, I spotted a large machichi tree with branches that stretched out over the ground. This was the same kind of tree I had climbed in the pueblo. The branches near the ground were too big to break, but I knew it would be easy to climb the tree to find thinner branches. I was even tempted to just crawl up and escape the camp for a moment, to feel the wind and solitude of a tree once again.

I hesitated a moment and then forced myself to

167

turn away and hike even farther from camp, honoring my vow to never again be a Tree Girl. Tree Girl was a coward who let her family die. Tree Girl was a coward who sat in a tree and let a whole pueblo die. I would never again climb a tree. Tree Girl was gone forever.

For the next two hours I searched, paying the price for not being a Tree Girl. Finally, at dusk, I found two half-rotted and twisted lengths of wood far from camp. I carried them back to the grandmothers. Carmen waved hello to me. Rosa took the long branches from my arms. "You were gone so long, I was making arrangements for your funeral," she said.

Using rocks to hold the edge of the plastic tarp to the hard dry ground, I dug holes and anchored the branches upright into the dry earth to form a rough tent for the grandmothers. Rosa and Carmen watched me and helped to stretch the tarp between the rocks and upright branches like a drum so rain wouldn't pool. This would serve as a shelter for all three of us.

It was dark by the time I finished, and the old women's hollow stares told me that hunger dug at their frail stomachs, but they refused to complain. Their pride wouldn't allow them to ask me for food.

"I'll try to find you food tonight," I told them as they thanked me again and again for the shelter.

"Maybe it isn't safe for you to go out in the dark," Carmen said.

"And maybe it isn't safe to starve to death," I replied.

CHAPTER TWELVE

W hen I finally returned to our camp, the old Kakchikel grandmothers were already under the tarp, asleep on the hard ground. They stirred restlessly in their sleep, but I didn't wake them. Sleep was their best escape from hunger and from the pain of memories. I had collected corn flour and rice along with some beans. I hoped that in the morning Carmen and Rosa would cook the beans and make tortillas on one of the small fires that sprang up around camp.

My own stomach was still knotted with hunger as I crawled under the tarp beside the old women to sleep. The day had left me exhausted, and quickly I fell into my own restless sleep.

When I woke, Carmen and Rosa were already up. They had found the food I collected the night before, and somewhere they had also found a pan and some water to boil the beans and make tortillas. To start their fire, they had borrowed flames from someone else's fire. Rosa met me as I crawled from the tent and she handed me a couple of warm tortillas. "Thank you for the food," she said.

I nodded and gulped down the tortillas. These were the first warm tortillas I had eaten in more than two months. I thanked the grandmothers and set out to find food for our next meal. "We'll look for food also," Carmen called after me.

I realized that without meaning to, I had accepted a new responsibility, and it troubled me. I didn't want anyone to depend on me, and I didn't want to depend on anyone. I left without answering Carmen, knowing that survival now consumed every waking minute of my life and forced me to wander constantly through the camp in search of food, clothes, and blankets.

I never knew when a truck might arrive. One deadly

fact remained. There wasn't enough food for everyone. If I found food for myself and the old women, then somewhere that night others would sleep hungry. If I survived one more day, someone else would die because I lived.

The San Miguel camp could have used ten times as much food and supplies, and the one thing we needed most of all, the trucks could not bring us: hope. Hope that the war might end soon, and hope that family would return. Many in the camp would have survived if they could have found hope, but with time, many gave up. I watched them sitting alone with vacant eyes, staring away from the camp to a place millions of miles away, a place where they would soon go. Sadly, some escaped by killing themselves. I saw their bodies, wrists cut wide open by jagged broken bottles that lay beside them on the ground.

Most of us kept to ourselves, not trusting those around us and not wanting to develop friendships that might soon be lost. We built small isolated worlds of memories, anger, and bitterness. And each refugee in camp avoided reality in a different way.

173

To hide their grief and fear, some parents in camp showed anger toward their children. Other refugees simply gave up and quit looking for food. My way of escaping reality was to occupy myself every waking moment of each day, leaving little time for memories or reflection. I feared that if I allowed memories into my mind, I, too, would become one of those who quit eating.

Each night the kindness of death found more of the refugees, and with the coming of morning their lifeless bodies were discovered motionless on the ground, as if caught in sleep.

Like most, I tried to ignore the dead resting on the ground around the camp. They were simply shapes, sad curiosities with a bad odor. To acknowledge the dead was to acknowledge the possibility that tomorrow I might be among them. I feared that morning when I would be too weak to search for food. That day it would be my turn to die. So each evening, when the Mexican workers came through camp wearing masks, picking up the dead with a truck, I looked away.

Some refugees in our part of camp tried to manufacture hope by sitting around a small fire each night sharing what they knew of the United States of America. On days when I was lucky enough to have found food, I would sit and listen to them talk about the heaven they called the United States.

"I have a cousin who lives in Los Angeles," one refugee said, gazing wistfully up at the stars as if recalling a dream. "He tells me that in the United States of America even the poor have cars and live in buildings with windows and doors."

"They say that the poor keep their food cold in electric refrigerators," another refugee added. "Their water runs from faucets, clean and pure, and even the poorest Americans have toilets that flush away their dung."

The refugees would talk for hours about leaving the camp and trying to make it north through Mexico to America. "The United States border is much harder to cross than the border we crossed to enter Mexico," one old man explained. "You need men called *coyotes* to smuggle you across. The coyotes are very dangerous men who charge much money."

"Yes, but it's worth it," a woman added. "In the United States there are hospitals to care for the poor and hungry."

One night I noticed a young man with glasses sitting and listening quietly to everyone telling stories about America. As the fire died down, the young man seemed to grow impatient. He suddenly spoke. "If it weren't for the Americans," he said, "the soldiers would never have attacked our cantóns."

Everybody sat in silence. It was as if the storytellers' dreams had been doused with cold water. "It's getting late," one woman complained.

"Yes, it's late," said another, as she stood to leave. I continued sitting there in the darkness as most of the others wandered back to their shelters. The young man with glasses remained sitting on the ground.

"Is it true what you said about the Americans?" I asked.

He nodded. "I was in the Guatemalan military. The United States made the guns that shot our families. They made the helicopters that destroy our peaceful skies. The comandantes that have led the massacres were trained in the United States of America."

"How many massacres have there been?" I asked.

The man waved his hand in a circle at the camp. "Enough to cause this," he said. "And this is only one of many camps. There have been hundreds and hundreds of massacres. This war is nothing short of genocide. Whole generations of Indios are being destroyed. Even here, we're still not safe. Guatemalan soldiers, *Kaibiles*, have crossed the border to our east and massacred many in other refugee camps."

"Don't the Mexican officials stop them?" I asked.

The young man shook his head. "They just stand and watch the Kaibiles commit their murders."

"So the Mexicans are as much to blame as the Americans?" questioned an older man.

"The Americans have armed and trained the Kaibiles."

"It can't be true what you say about the United States," I argued. "Many Americans help us here in the camp. They send much of the supplies we receive."

"You speak of American citizens," the young man said. "Not the American government. Most Americans don't know what their government does. They don't want to know," he added.

The young man bit at his lip as I sat thinking about what he had said. I didn't know if the stories about the poor in the United States of America were exaggerated, but I had to admit that they sounded wonderful. Still, how was it possible for a country to be so great and yet allow for the massacres in our cantóns and pueblos?

The young man reached out his hand to me. "I'm Mario Salvador," he said. "What's your name?"

"I'm Gabriela Flores," I replied. "What did you do after leaving the military?"

"I became a teacher."

I visited with Mario that night until the cold was too much to bear. When I finally slept, I dreamed of guns and helicopters. I dreamed of the new teacher I had met, and as always, I dreamed of a little girl who once cuddled by my side and called me Mamí.

Because I went to bed late, I slept until after the sun came up. It surprised me to see Rosa still lying asleep beside me when I rose. I looked out and saw

Carmen cooking, crouched over a small fire in front of our shelter. I stared again at Rosa and sensed a strange stillness. I reached and touched her back. Then I squeezed her shoulder. "Rosa, wake up," I said, realizing at that moment that she was dead. I drew in a slow, deliberate breath. "Rosa is dead," I called to Carmen.

Carmen came to my side, wiping her eyes and shaking her head. "I'll stay with her until the truck arrives," she said.

"We'll stay together," I said. "Was she sick?"

Carmen shook her head.

"Then why did she die?" I asked. "Maybe I could have found her a little more food."

Carmen shook her head again. "You couldn't have stopped Rosa's death."

I said a quiet prayer as I waited beside Rosa, knowing even as I mouthed the words that prayers didn't work anymore, not in a refugee camp. I blamed Rosa's death on the soldiers, just as I blamed them for the deaths they caused with their bullets.

I wanted to bury Rosa, but I knew refugees weren't

allowed to bury any of the dead. Rosa would have to wait for the Mexican workers who wore masks to come with the truck. Rosa's body would be stacked like firewood with other bodies under a tarp on a truck, only to be burned and buried in a common grave far from camp. This was done to stop the spread of disease and epidemics.

In the past, I had been able to ignore the removal of bodies, but that day I could not. When the truck arrived, I insisted on helping carry Rosa's body. Her thin frame weighed less than a jug of water as we carried her to the truck. I bent and kissed her forehead gently before workers heaved her body on top of the rest. It was a kiss that should have come from her husband or her children.

Before Rosa's death, I had already worked hard to help care for the old women. Now I drove myself even harder, fighting to escape my thoughts. I obsessed over tasks, quitting only when my weary body collapsed in sleep. I was a terrified child, running from myself in the only way I knew, afraid that maybe tomorrow morning the Mexican workers would carry away the small, thin body of a homely girl named Gabriela.

"Don't work so hard," Carmen scolded me when-ever she found me exhausted. "We have enough food to eat." I always nodded, but I ignored her words.

Each day more refugees straggled into the camp, look-ing as if they arrived from the grave, their gaunt faces only vague masks of what had once been happy chil-dren, proud parents, or dignified elders. Each step of the long trail had robbed them of another shard of their identity, their hopes, their culture, their dreams, and their pride. Now they wandered into the camp not as individuals, but simply as faceless refugees searching for food and shelter. Their ragged clothes and desper-ate stares blended with all the rest.

Perhaps that's why I failed to recognize the small girl when I first saw her two months after I arrived. It was late evening as I stood in the long water line, grasping two plastic jugs. The large tanker truck threat-ened to run out of water before my turn arrived. Already the pressure of the spigot had weakened into a thin stream. As I waited, a group of fifteen or twenty refugees wandered into camp. Everyone in line glanced at the new arrivals with idle curiosity. As I returned my gaze to the truck, something about the group caused me to glance back.

Several young girls had wandered in with the new refugees. One in particular, who stood turned away from me, had skinny legs that bowed slightly, shoulders that rounded, and long black hair that hung nearly to her waist. Her blue dress was unfamiliar and she kept looking away, but I watched her as the group passed, hoping she would turn or glance my way.

"Alicia!" I called out.

Still the girl failed to turn.

"Alicia!" I yelled more loudly.

The girl turned and stared at me with large searching eyes. My breath stopped in my chest and the empty water jugs dropped from my hands. I took two hesitant steps forward and then broke into a fast run.

"Alicia! Alicia! Alicia!" I screamed.

CHAPTER THIRTEEN

The stunned little girl stared at me with big eyes, and I fell to my knees and hugged her desperately. The world blurred as I burst into tears. "Alicia, Alicia," I sobbed.

Alicia hugged me back, clinging to me. She was dirty beyond belief, and her tangled black hair was like that of a thousand other children in the camp. But this wasn't just one of the other children. This was my sister, and I kept hugging her until a hand touched my shoulder and I looked up.

A large woman stood over me with a small baby cradled in her arms. "How do you know this girl?" the woman asked accusingly.

I stood and lifted Alicia into my arms and spoke joyfully. "I'm Gabriela. This is my little sister, Alicia."

The woman looked at me as if she had seen a ghost. "You're Gabriela?"

I nodded.

"I'm María," the large woman said.

"Where did you find my sister?" I asked.

"Back in Guatemala, far south of the border. One day as I walked to market, I heard shooting ahead of me in the pueblo. People screamed, and I knew it was the soldiers. When I turned to run, I heard a baby cry. I found this girl and this baby hiding alone behind some thick shrubs. The baby was almost dead, so I took them both with me away from the pueblo and back to our cantón."

I looked at the child in the woman's arms. "Is that the baby?"

The woman nodded. "She almost died. Is she your sister, too?"

I shook my head in disbelief, staring at the squirming infant. "No," I said. "I helped her to be born, but I think her mother died. I don't know, because the soldiers came and I had to run."

"Did you see the massacre?" María asked.

I nodded.

"How did you survive? You must have been very brave," she said.

I felt new shame. "I hid," I said, unwilling to talk any more of that day. I looked at the big woman, her skin dusty and cracked from the hot sun. Her hollowed face and sunken eyes told of how hard her long journey had been. "It'll be dark soon," I said. "I can help you find a place to sleep."

"Thank you, Gabriela," the woman said.

"Can I carry the baby?" I asked, lowering Alicia to the ground.

Maria looked relieved as she handed me the small infant that had grown much since birth. She was dirty and her upper lip was crusted from a runny nose, but her skin was no longer pale. A brightness glowed in her eyes.

My mind struggled with what was happening. It didn't seem possible that this could be the same baby I had helped to deliver. "Follow me," I said, leading Maria through the camp. Alicia clung tightly to my corte.

Carmen frowned when I walked into camp carrying a baby, and followed by a woman and a little girl. Already life was difficult. To feed this many more mouths might be impossible.

"Carmen, this is my sister and the baby I told you I helped to be born. María found them and brought them here."

Carmen extended her hand, concern heavy on her face.

"I'll find extra food," I said, feeling guilty.

"*All* of us will need to work harder," Carmen said, not hiding the intent and sharpness of her words.

I looked at our small shelter. María was much bigger than Rosa had been. And now we also had a young girl and a baby. I hoped Carmen wouldn't mind. I went to her alone. "Letting María stay with us was the kind thing to do," I said.

"It's okay," Carmen said. "Just remember, Gabriela. Kindness can kill you in this place."

186

I nodded and left María and the baby in camp, and took Alicia with me to find food.

Everywhere we went, Alicia clung to me. Even when she helped me to carry rice and bread, she held to me with one hand. Some of the aid workers smiled and tried to play with Alicia, but she remained silent and hid behind my corte.

That night after all of us had eaten something, we sat together on the ground beside our shelter, talking as I brushed Alicia's long hair. "Something's wrong with Alicia's voice," I explained to Carmen. "She can't speak anymore."

María shook her head. "Your sister only refuses to speak. I've heard her cry out your name, Gabriela, when she's dreaming. That's why it surprised me so much when you told me your name today. Somehow Alicia needs to find her voice when she's awake."

While we spoke, Alicia stared at the ground. I turned to María. "Do you mind if I hold the baby?"

María smiled and handed the baby girl to me. I rocked her gently in my arms as I explained to María all that had happened.

When I finished, María told me her story. "Soldiers came to our cantón six weeks after the massacre in the pueblo," she said. "Alicia and the baby were in the field with me that day, so I took them and fled north toward Mexico. We could not even return to our home first."

As María spoke, I cuddled the sleeping baby closely to my chest, proud that I had helped bring her into the world. "Have you given the baby a name yet?" I asked.

María shook her head. "We thought some mother had already named her, so we simply called her Little One."

"There was never time to give her a name," I said.

María thought a moment. "If the baby has no name yet, maybe we should call her *Milagro*. It's a miracle that she survived when so many others died."

I nodded in the dark. "Milagro is a good name," I said. "Our little miracle." What had happened to Milagro truly was a miracle. I looked down at the little infant and also at Alicia cuddled by my side, and I pulled them both closer. "Milagro's mother would have liked that name," I said.

I reached out and ran my fingers through Alicia's long black hair. This day had brought me another miracle. "I'll never leave you again," I whispered to Alicia, fearful that I might be making another false promise.

With three more bodies to feed, I pushed myself even harder to find food. Alicia walked everywhere with me, and always I had to make sure she was safe. María watched the baby and tried to find special foods for her.

Whenever I tried talking to Alicia, I saw her eyes glimmer with thoughts, but she barricaded those thoughts behind silence. Each night in camp, she sat, digging with a small stick in the ground, or rocking back and forth as she gazed away toward some other section of camp or toward someplace known only to her.

It was more work feeding the five of us, but we survived. In the months after Alicia's return, the camp grew even more crowded. It hurt the most to watch the children, knowing that the war hadn't allowed them a childhood. They couldn't cry or play or laugh or shout. They feared each new day, mindful that they must always be still or die. Now those same children huddled alone, gazing at the world around them with frightened eyes. In the Ixil section, the Mam section, the Kakchikel, in our Quiché section, and in other parts of camp, mothers kept their children close to their sides and hushed their cries.

Alicia behaved the same way, clinging always to my side, refusing to smile, laugh, or speak. When she thought no one watched, she took a stick and hit at the ground. Sometimes she hit the ground so hard that her small knuckles bled. Her silence failed to hide the fear and hurt and the anger that she struggled with. Night after night I watched Alicia struggle with her feelings and thoughts, and I felt helpless.

One afternoon I picked up some old cloth rags from beside the dirt road and wound them tightly to make a small ball. I took the ball and rolled it to Alicia. At first she sat and stared at it, but after much coaxing she finally pushed it back toward me. After that it was nearly a week before she stood and kicked the ball, and still another week before she allowed herself to chase the ball.

Other children peeked out from behind their

mothers' cortes and watched us. Slowly Alicia began to play, trying to keep the ball away from me or chasing me, but still she remained hidden inside her silent world without expression.

Each day I made time for play, even when we could find no food. We played in the mornings early before the heat came, and some days we also played in the evening after the sun had set. Alicia sometimes allowed a grunt when she kicked the ball, but nothing more.

One evening as Alicia and I chased each other, kicking the ball, a young boy approached. He walked slowly toward us, as if unable to resist the temptation of play. I kicked the rag ball to him, and he reluctantly kicked it back. When I kicked the ball again, it rolled past him. He stared at it with a somber face for a moment, then walked slowly after the ball and kicked it back once again. After that, the boy, Alfredo, returned to kick the ball with us whenever he saw us playing. It was three days before he ran for the first time. It was longer yet before he laughed.

Still the other children only watched.

The next child to join us was a tall, skinny girl named Laura. I doubted she was more than eleven or twelve, but her size and her haunted, serious eyes made her appear older. She kicked the ball with hesitant bunts, clenching her fists and biting at her lip in anger whenever the ball got away from her.

Kicking the ball straight wasn't important. Smiling was. Purposely I pretended to miss the ball each time I kicked, or I pretended to fall. Finally a faint smile creased Laura's lips. It was hard for me to laugh and act happy when inside I felt like crying, but it was good to see guarded smiles steal across the faces of those children who played and those who watched.

Each week more children found the courage to join us, and each day they kicked the rag ball harder and harder. Sometimes their kicks were fierce. It hurt me to think what memories caused such anger. Seldom did laughs or shouts escape their mouths, and then only by accident.

Because the rag ball kept shredding, I finally approached one of the aid workers who had come to recognize me. I gathered my courage and asked her, "Is there anyplace you can get us a ball?"

The American aid worker shook her head. "This isn't a playground. This is a refugee camp."

"The children need to learn how to be happy again," I argued, afraid I might make the woman mad. "To be happy they must play, and to play we need a good ball."

"What the camp needs is more medicine and food," the woman said firmly.

"A ball is medicine," I argued stubbornly. "It makes children happy again."

The woman finally relented and promised, "I'll see what I can do."

"Thank you," I said.

Each day I returned and asked the woman, "Did you find a ball yet?"

Each day she shook her head. "I'm trying," she said.

"Can you try harder?" I begged one day. "The children need to be happy today, not tomorrow. Please."

Maybe she wished to rid herself of me, I don't know, but the next day when I returned, the woman went to the cab of her van and brought back a real leather football. She called it a soccer ball.

"Where did this come from?" I asked.

She smiled. "From one of the other aid workers, who doesn't know yet that he donated it. Take care of this ball. There won't be another one."

"I will, I will," I promised.

I felt like the richest person in the world that evening when I presented the children with a real leather ball. Word spread quickly, and children from other parts of the camp came to play with us. To make sure the ball wasn't stolen, I left it with María when it wasn't being used. Nothing was safe if left unattended in the refugee camp. If María was too busy cooking or caring for Milagro, I carried the ball myself, and each night I slept with Alicia on one side of me and the ball on the other side. It meant too much to all of us for me to let it out of my sight.

Sometimes Milagro sat for hours with the ball between her small pudgy legs, rolling it forward and back between her knees. María and I always made time to play games with Milagro. We were her mothers now, smothering her with attention and extra food. She loved when I found bullion cubes for her to suck on. Her dimpled cheeks and curls couldn't hide her strong will. All of her short life she had needed to be strong.

Alicia remained mute, stubbornly refusing to open her guarded world. I did find hope, however, when one night an old stray cat wandered through camp looking for scraps. Carrying a stick, Alicia walked deliberately up to the cat and crouched. I feared she would hit the animal, but instead she reached and gently stroked the small cat. She looked over her shoulder to make sure no one watched.

After that, Alicia saved a scrap of food each day. She would approach the cat when she thought nobody watched. We all learned to pretend we were busy with some chore when the cat wandered into camp.

In time, Carmen and María became close friends, sharing food and helping each other to gather firewood. I was nearly sixteen then, and realized that the war could continue on for months or years. None of us had wanted the camp to become our home, but we had no choice.

Maybe for this reason I, too, enjoyed sitting in the

evening and listening to refugees from our section of camp speak of other places, especially the United States of America. I liked to go and listen to talk about the great opportunities that existed outside of our hole of filth. I also hoped to see the teacher, Mario Salvador, again. Mario never spoke much, but he always had a smile for me, and I could tell that others respected his few words as I did.

No matter what was said each night about escaping to the United States, our discussions always ended with someone reminding the rest of us, "It's illegal and dangerous, and you'll need money."

For me, life was already dangerous, and earning money in a refugee camp was impossible because nobody had any. We had no fields to grow corn or coffee, nor had we any marketplace to sell anything. Everything in camp was begged or traded for, if not stolen. And where could we go for hope? Hope was not something to be handed out from the back of a truck like rice or beans.

CHAPTER FOURTEEN

As the months passed in camp, new refugees arrived with fresh stories of more military death squads and new massacres in the cantóns and pueblos back in Guatemala. Each day more people were being taken from their homes never to be seen again, and more refugees on the trail were coming under attack by the soldiers. Still, we feared that the Guatemalan Kaibiles would soon attack our camp in Mexico.

We lived in fear, but by year's end the number of trucks arriving with donated food and supplies had more than doubled. Aid workers began construction on two rows of sheet metal buildings for the oldest and the sickest refugees. Still, it was dangerous collecting food. Strong people muscled their way to the front of every crowd, while the old and the weak watched help-lessly. Sometimes whole families waited all day only to watch the last truck drive away empty.

One day I ran to an arriving truck. Before a crowd formed, the driver crawled from the cab. He carried a stick, and as I watched, he scraped a long line in the dirt from the truck out across the open ground. "I give food only to people who stand on this line," the driver shouted.

At first refugees ran and jostled for positions on the line, but soon everyone waited patiently. I liked what the driver had done. Usually the old and sick never had a chance. Until that day, the only place a line formed was at the water truck, because they used a single faucet.

Other drivers must have seen what happened. Soon, all trucks refused to unload unless refugees formed a line. When this happened, lines began form-ing even before the trucks arrived. Overnight, collect-ing food ceased to take up all of my time. For the first time, I noticed refugees standing or sitting around camp, visiting with one another.

With the extra time, I found myself restless, unable to run from my emotions and thoughts by working every waking hour. In the evenings I took Alicia with me when I went to listen to the men talk about life outside the camp. Because of my age, and because I was a female, I might as well have been invisible during these discussions, but on the nights that Mario Salvador stayed later than the rest, I would sit and talk with him. He reminded me of Manuel, though younger.

Because of Mario, I found new hope in the future. Mario never talked about toilets that flushed or swimming pools. He spoke about the children and the tragedies that war brought to them. He spoke of the Indios and of self-worth. For the first time, I allowed myself to recount events from the night of my quinceañera. I shared memories of the night I returned to our cantón from market, and I allowed myself to speak of the massacre in the pueblo. Mario listened to me patiently, nodding kindly to show his understanding.

199

He even wept quietly at times.

Seldom did Mario speak of himself except to say that he had lost his wife to the soldiers. "I loved her very much," he told me.

One night I asked him, "When do you think the war will end?"

"Which war?" he replied.

"I know only about the one with the soldiers and the guerrillas," I said.

Mario shook his head. "That's only one of many wars. For you, being a female is a war that you'll fight all of your life. For both of us, being Indio is a war we fought even before the soldiers came."

I nodded. I had been fighting so hard.

Mario continued speaking. "Three years ago, the rains failed to come where we lived. Our crops grew like fields of weeds. Finally, in desperation, my brother, Edgar, and my father, they decided to travel to the western coast to pick cotton for a season. This frightened me, because I'd heard how the rich Latinos treated the Indio.

"They rode for a whole day in the back of an overloaded truck to the coast. The *patrón* who owned the large farm where they worked, he treated my brother and father like dogs. They had worked for only a month when one day the patrón had airplanes spray chemicals on the fields without warning. Chemicals landed directly on Edgar and two other workers. When the spray cleared, the three couldn't breathe, and they gasped and held their hands to their faces.

"The patrón claimed he had personally warned the workers, but Father told me later the patrón wasn't even in the field that day. For three days Edgar's skin blistered and he struggled to breathe, so Father brought him home. For a month the curandero did everything she could to heal Edgar with herbs, but nothing helped. His breathing became very shallow and he finally died.

"We were helpless to do anything, because we were only Indios. Our voices and our lives meant less to the Latinos and to the government than even the dogs. I don't think the patrón would have ever sprayed his dogs. There was nothing we could do when Edgar died except bury him and say our prayers."

Mario stared at the ground as he spoke, his voice growing hard like mud in the hot sun. "After Edgar's death Father returned to the farm, but the patrón refused to meet with him. The patrón claimed that Father was a troublemaker and that if he didn't leave right away, he would be arrested. And so Father left without even an apology from the man who had killed his son. An Indio has no right to complain."

"I'm sorry," I said.

Mario nodded. "We have many wars and many enemies," he said.

Because of our talk that night, I found myself the next day thinking about my people, the Indios, while I stood in line waiting for water. Here in the camp, a whole generation of children was growing up with no education of any kind. They weren't learning to weave, plant, or cook. Nor were they learning to read or write. They were growing up as beggars, knowing only the dirty hand-to-mouth existence of a refugee camp. That day, waiting in line, an idea formed in my mind.

One week later, as Mario and I sat talking, I suggested my idea. "What do you think about starting a school for the children?"

Mario looked at me to see if I was serious.

"We already have a teacher," I added with a smile. "This is our home now, and we might be here for years. The children still need to be educated. Otherwise, being Indio will always be a shameful thing."

Mario nodded. "You're right. Children grow up with nothing if they don't learn pride and dignity."

I knew at that moment that Mario Salvador was a good teacher. A good teacher didn't criticize an idea simply because it came from a young woman instead of from him. A good teacher embraced new ideas, just as Manuel always had.

We talked long that night about our new school. Mario agreed that he would be the teacher and I would help him with the younger students. We hoped we could find some paper and pencils. After having found a ball, I felt certain that I could find school supplies.

"It may take a while before children start coming to the school," Mario warned.

"Many things take a while," I said. "Even starvation takes a while."

Mario smiled at me. "I know now why you survived

the massacres. You were too stubborn to die."

I laughed, trying to ignore the lingering feeling that I had survived only because I was a coward.

By the end of that week, I had made it known around the Quiché section of camp that a school would be starting. I encouraged parents to come as well. Many children would be too afraid to come alone, although by now many knew me and knew each other from playing with the ball.

Our school started in October, a time of heavy rains in the Chiapas area of Mexico, and a steady downpour greeted our first day of school. Children walked through ankle-deep mud to join us. Sitting around, covered with pieces of plastic or cardboard, wasn't as easy as learning in a schoolroom with a blackboard and desk, but it was better than learning nothing and abandoning hope.

Our first students huddled together, their eyes filled with fear and distrust. Still, their curiosity had brought them to us. Standing with no cover, Mario welcomed the small group of thirty children and an equal number of parents that had showed. Then he did something that surprised me. He walked to the side of the group and picked up off the ground an old and flattened carcass of a dead rat. "What is this?" he said, waving the dead animal at the children.

Some children screamed and some laughed.

"It's a baby soldier," Mario said.

The children and parents laughed nervously.

"Tell me—what weighs one hundred and fifty pounds but runs from a mouse?" Mario asked. When nobody guessed, Mario answered, "A soldier without his gun."

Telling "bad-soldier jokes" was Mario's way of helping the refugees to confront and fight back against the monsters that had victimized them so tragically. Within minutes, Mario had others making up their own bad-soldier jokes.

"What is this?" a little boy named Pedro asked, flapping his arms and jumping in circles.

We all shrugged our shoulders.

"It's a soldier without his helicopter."

Everybody laughed at the child's joke.

One parent asked, "What do you get when you

mix a pig and a soldier?"

"An ugly pig," one of the children shouted.

"No," the parent said. "Nothing. Pigs don't like soldiers either."

Some jokes carried the sad and cruel irony of truth and crowded too close to my memories.

"What does a soldier do when he goes to confession?" one mother asked. She answered with "Nothing, he just sits there alone because he's already killed the priest."

After the bad-soldier jokes, Mario found out with playful questions how much each child already knew. Most couldn't read or write, and so we started by learning the alphabet. "A, B, C, D, E," we recited. Manuel used an old plank and some charcoal from the fire to make letters. It became a game for each child to learn how to spell and recognize their own name and the names of others.

To encourage more children to attend the school, I announced, "Starting today, only those children who attend school can play with the leather ball."

When the school first started, I'd been in camp

nearly a year and a half. Many changes had occurred, but the most important change for me was the sound of the shouts and laughter of children that had begun to fill the air. I continued to push many things from my mind, but one by one the children around me began to make their way inside my heart. There was little Isabel, who had escaped her cantón with only her uncle, Jose. And there was Felipe, who played constant tricks on everybody he met. I came to love Miguel, and Luci, and Oscar, and many more. Each of them had their own unique and tragic stories. Each of them came with their problems, but they also brought their potential.

Alicia sat quietly at school each day. She was nearly six, and some days she held Milagro on her lap like a big sister. She still refused to speak, but I had begun to accept her silence. In camp we had found other tarps, so each of us had our own shelter with ropes and sawn boards to hold up the fronts. Alicia and I slept together.

Each day the children learned more in school, and I spent more hours helping Mario to teach them.

When the aid workers heard about our little school, they made sure we received paper and pencils. I felt a certain satisfaction working with the students. I had promised my parents to someday teach others what I had learned. At least I was honoring one of my promises.

I was feeling stronger with each passing week, until Mario came to me one cloudy and windy afternoon three months after school had begun. The children had finished their lessons for the day and were kicking the ball in the rain. Already small cooking fires flickered around the dirty camp, hissing and sparking with the rain. I was crouched beside our fire, making tortillas, when Mario's soft voice surprised me from behind.

"Gabriela, I'm leaving the camp," he said.

CHAPTER FIFTEEN

Mario's words struck me like a fist, and he saw the shock in my eyes. "I'm returning to Guatemala to fight with the guerrillas and the resistance," he said.

"I don't understand," I stuttered, struggling to comprehend his words. "What about the children?"

"You can teach them," he said. "Fighting with the guerrillas against the soldiers is the best way I can help my country. The soldiers have become an evil force, more evil than anybody ever imagined."

"When did you decide this?" I asked.

"When does a cup become full?" Mario said. "This

cup has been filling for a long time. More and more Indios have joined the resistance, and I now believe that is our only hope."

"And when are you leaving?" I asked.

"Now," he said quietly.

I broke down in tears and hugged Mario. "Can I go with you?" I pleaded.

He took my face in his hands and kissed my forehead gently. "Your place is here with the children. Be the best teacher you can. You're a very special person. Maybe someday I will see you again."

And then, as suddenly as he had appeared, Mario turned and walked away, throwing my world into complete confusion. Mario had no right to leave. Teaching the children was a dream that he and I had shared. It wasn't my dream alone. I didn't want the school to be my responsibility. And what if Mario was hurt or killed?

Without thinking, I called Alicia to my side. "We're leaving also," I said, not knowing where we would go. I hadn't admitted it, but Mario had been my only reason for staying in the San Miguel refugee camp. Now that he was leaving, I suddenly wanted to leave also. Without Mario, I didn't want to teach the children. Somewhere I would find a different home. I felt a sudden emptiness inside of me. I craved to live again as I once had as a child in the cantón. I missed my old life, and I missed my family. I wanted to return to happier times before the soldiers and before the massacres.

Alicia watched me with big, curious eyes as I rushed around taking down our tarp and folding up my old blanket. As I worked, I justified leaving in my mind. This camp had nearly destroyed my pride and dignity. Our cantón had been clean, not dirty with human waste and apathy. Our homes in Guatemala had lush green forests and mountain streams and colorful birds, with roosters crowing before daybreak. I dearly missed the planting season, when everyone, even the children, helped to carefully place seeds into the womb of our mother earth. Those were the memories of my heart.

But even as I wrapped tortillas into my shawl, I knew my memories were only simple and familiar things that I craved to relive. They were like stories that old men tell to help recall their youth. They were no longer real.

I was glad that María, Carmen, and Milagro weren't in camp. They would have made it much harder to leave. I did write them a note that said simply, "I've left to find a home."

Thoughts kept boiling in my mind as I finished preparing. Only one thing was real in my life: this moment. I was a refugee in another country, with no rights, no future, and little respect. But I didn't plan on going to the United States of America.

My world back in the cantón had been the earth and sky and those things that nature provided. The sun was my father. My mother was the moon and the earth. All that I needed, the sky and the earth provided.

The gringos didn't know this same mother or father. They knew only a world of cars and computers and televisions, the things that they had created. The land they lived on didn't hold the sacred ashes of their ancestors or the sacred fluids of their children. I knew that I would never understand the path I followed into the future if I failed to understand the path of the ancients. It seemed very sad to me to think that some would so quickly trade the rich traditions of our Mayan past for the modern conveniences of a future in America.

With everything I owned wrapped inside a shawl on my back, I took Alicia's hand and walked quickly from the camp. My restlessness was that of a lost person who searches for a home that no longer exists. I was confused and torn between memories and dreams, between hope and fear. Anger and dissatisfaction demanded that I leave the camp, but I didn't know where leaving would take me.

Leaving frightened me greatly, but not as much as staying. I had no money, and Alicia and I would have to travel however we could, walking or begging rides in the backs of trucks. Still, I was determined to do anything I had to.

The tortillas I'd made would last me for a few days, and after that, life promised little. Mexico was a very large country, and all that I owned I carried with me. My only connection to the past was a mute six-year-old sister who depended on me for everything. It frightened me that once again everything familiar was being torn away and separated from my life. María, Carmen, little Milagro, all the children I'd helped, and yes, those who had helped me, all would soon fade to memories in my mind.

I knew María and Carmen would be hurt by my sudden leaving, but I wasn't their daughter. What about their dreams? Their futures? Did they want a refugee camp to be their home forever? In any case, they would survive without me. As for the school-children, they weren't mine. Nor was Milagro, even though I had helped to care for her. I would miss little Milagro, but María would care for her. Alicia was my only real family, and I was willing to sacrifice every-thing to find a place we could truly call home.

To reach the highway, I needed to walk through the middle of camp. I walked rapidly among the tarps, the slatted wood lean-tos, and the plastic tents that now made up the San Miguel refugee camp. Much had changed from that day when I first arrived nearly two years earlier. Life was still hard, but children now laughed and shouted. People waited patiently in lines for supplies that were brought to their section of camp. The dead-body trucks no longer drove through camp each morning. They even had a small clinic set up in a trailer. The line to see the nurses sometimes stretched far across the camp.

"Hello, Gabriela," people called as we walked from the camp.

"Gabriela, come play with us," the children called.

"Maybe tomorrow," I called back.

Today, it seemed that everybody recognized me. They waved and called out as I walked faster to escape.

"Come here, Gabriela," one woman called to me. "Look at this."

Because I had passed very near to the woman, Vera, I reluctantly stopped to watch her son writing with a pencil on a piece of paper. In big block letters he had spelled out T H O M A S. He looked up at me and smiled through missing front teeth. "Thomas," he said to me. "I can write my own name."

"Very good," I said. "You've worked so hard."

"No," said his mother. "It's you who has worked hard. It's you who started the school and brought the teacher and the children together. Because of you we have a school. That's why Thomas can write his name. Thank you."

"Tomorrow I want to learn my last name," Thomas said. "Will you teach me?"

I fought back the emotions churning up inside of me. This was a refugee camp full of dreamers who lived on false hope. I was leaving this place and following real hope. There was nothing wrong with wanting to find someplace that could be a real home for Alicia and me. But even as I struggled with my emotions, I still didn't know where or what home was.

I nodded to Thomas, but I lied. I was leaving.

When I reached the edge of camp, it was almost dark and I didn't know where to spend the night. It would be dangerous to travel the road at this time. Without giving my decision much thought, I walked with Alicia out away from camp toward a large machichi tree on a nearby hill. After dark, we would sleep under that tree, then rise early before dawn and begin our journey to another place.

When Alicia and I arrived at the machichi tree, I

opened my shawl and spread the worn blanket on the ground beneath the broad-reaching branches. Angry thoughts smoldered inside of me. Leaving the camp had been so much harder than I imagined, but I kept telling myself that leaving was the right thing to do, especially since Mario had left.

I lowered myself onto the blanket. "Come lie down beside me," I told Alicia, my voice demanding.

Alicia disobeyed my words. She walked to the tree and sat on the hard ground apart from me, looking up through the branches of the machichi tree into the gathering darkness. Already a few stars tried to peek down at us.

"Come sleep with me," I told Alicia once again, speaking more sharply. "Tomorrow we begin a long and dangerous journey. We need to get sleep."

Still Alicia ignored me, sitting alone and staring up.

I stood angrily to bring Alicia to my side, but then stopped myself. Tonight Alicia had isolated herself from the world with more than silence, and her distance left me feeling even more alone myself. I didn't want to admit that I needed companionship. Back in camp I would have been surrounded by those I knew, but I wanted more than a refugee camp for a home. I wanted more for my future than sleeping under a tarp, searching and scrounging each day for handouts. Alicia feared life, but I was not afraid to try and find us a better one.

I removed the brush from under my huipil and sat quietly behind Alicia. Gently I began stroking her long black hair. "Let's have a talk," I said quietly.

Alicia's silence left plenty of space for my words.

"I know you're scared," I said. "But you can't run from what's happened by not speaking. If you don't speak, you'll trap all of those bad memories inside of you forever."

Alicia looked down at her lap and started picking at her fingernails.

"You can't hide from what I'm saying by pretending not to listen," I added, finding it difficult to speak, as if I, too, were hiding from something. I kept brushing her long hair. "Can't you see?" I pleaded. "If you don't speak, you'll never heal. Some people run with their feet when they're scared, but if you don't speak, your silence will keep you running forever." My voice trembled as I spoke. Suddenly, my own words made me feel awkward and uncomfortable.

Alicia looked back up at the branches. Slowly she stood, pulling her hair away from my stroking brush. She reached out deliberately and touched the tree. Without looking back, she stepped up on an exposed root and reached her little arms toward a branch above her head.

"Don't climb the tree," I said, my voice sounding sharply again. "It's dangerous." But even as I spoke, I was ashamed of my words. I sounded like a worried grandmother.

Alicia turned to me in the dim light of dusk, her accusing eyes asking me why she shouldn't climb the machichi tree.

My mind struggled with unexplainable emotions as I studied her. I looked away toward the last shade of light on the horizon. I didn't want Alicia to see the tears filling my eyes. I, too, was afraid, more afraid then I had yet admitted. I had asked Alicia not to run from her fear, but this very evening I also ran from myself.

We were both trying to escape the past.

Slowly I stood and looked back at the camp. Darkness was settling fast, and already dim flames flickered in the distance. Yes, I, too, had been running, not by refusing to speak but by occupying every waking moment and never letting my mind be still. I also ran by trying to avoid getting too close to others and by always blaming myself for what happened. But I ran the most by refusing to ever again be a Tree Girl. That was my greatest betrayal.

Hesitantly I stepped to where Alicia stood looking up at the branch. My fear almost stopped me. What I thought of doing tested my courage more than facing any soldier's gun. I kneeled beside Alicia and pulled her to my chest and hugged her. "Do you want to be a Tree Girl?" I asked.

Alicia pushed away from me, her eyes showing her puzzlement.

"Here," I said, lifting her in my arms. "Do you want to sit in the tree?"

She nodded.

Carefully I lifted Alicia so that she could sit on the

lowest branch. "My little Tree Girl," I said, holding her with my arms as I remained firmly on the ground. I spoke quietly to my little sister. "When you climb a tree, it takes you closer to . . ." I stopped myself from finishing the sentence.

Alicia's small hand pulled up on mine, and my breath caught in my throat. My heart beat faster. If I resisted, how could I ever again face Alicia or forgive myself? No one but I would appreciate the consequence of my simply not moving. No one else would know my betrayal.

Again Alicia pulled up on my hand. I think that simple act made all the difference. Imperceptibly at first, I reached up, my heart pounding, my body trembling as if from fever. Then I gripped the branch. Deliberately I lifted my feet off the ground and pulled myself up beside Alicia. Emotions flooded through me, and I saw with tearful clearness Mamí and Papí and everyone I had ever loved and lost. I wept for my past, the past of the ancients and that of my ancestors, and for one brief moment I glimpsed the future, a future that held hope depending on what path I chose for myself that night.

Alicia looked over at my tears with haunting, innocent eyes.

"Tree Girls," I whispered to Alicia, "are very special. They're not cowards. They don't blame themselves for things they can't control. Tree Girls know that when they climb they might fall. But they know also that climbing lets them visit the birds. They're strong enough to face the bad in life in order to know the good. They're strong enough to face pain so that they can also know hope. They're willing to risk the ugliness of life in return for the beauty they find. Tree Girls find beauty when nobody else dares."

Alicia sat quietly on the branch, listening to me.

"Yes," I continued. "A Tree Girl is very special. But you can't be a Tree Girl if you run from what scares you. You're a Tree Girl only if you face the things that frighten you, and you must start by letting yourself speak."

Alicia stared at me, as if asking with her eyes, if I was also a Tree Girl. I ignored her gaze and kept speaking. I spoke words I had never spoken before. And even as I spoke, I knew I would be returning to the San Miguel refugee camp that night. I had survived the massacre not because I was a coward but because I was strong, and so that I could help others survive.

I once promised my parents that the education they had worked so hard to provide for me would be shared. I promised them that someday I would return and share my knowledge with other Quiché.

I needed to return to camp in order to keep that promise. Yes, before we slept that night I would return to the camp, and someday I would return to Guatemala to find the beauty that a young girl had left behind. The beauty I found would be a reflection of the beauty that already existed inside of me. Someday I would return to Guatemala and search for a special teacher named Mario. I would return to tell of the massacres, and I would return to find the songs of my people, songs left by the ancients, songs heard late at night when my soul was quiet and dared listen to the wind.

"A Tree Girl is someone who's willing to go home," I whispered to Alicia. "Not to someplace far away with running water and machines that keep food cold, but home to where we're needed and loved. You and I can be Tree Girls," I whispered to Alicia. "There are still ways for us to help others back in camp. Always there will be ways to help our people.

"Please help me, Alicia," I pleaded. "Antonio didn't sacrifice his life so that you could remain silent all of yours. Manuel didn't die so that I could leave my people and go to someplace where life is easy."

Alicia began pulling and twisting at her long hair, the way she often did when her thoughts grew troubled. But still her silence filled the night. I knew she didn't understand all of my words, but I think she understood when I said, "Alicia, we need to go back to María, Carmen, and Milagro, and to all the children. They're our family now. Wherever they are, that's where our home is. Here is where we belong."

I sat a long time on the branch, letting my mind and my heart accept this decision. Then I drew in a deep breath. "Yes, this is where we belong," I said, speaking to myself, to Alicia, and to the night sky that now bathed us in a warm darkness.

My little sister nodded, and then she also drew in a deep breath and looked up into the branches. "Can we climb higher?" she asked, her scratchy voice barely loud enough to be heard.

I gasped, and all of the world stopped at the sound of my sister's voice. Turning on the branch, I hugged Alicia hard, and in the peaceful silence that followed her words, I whispered in her ear, "Yes, we'll climb higher. Climbing a tree takes you closer to heaven."